Champagne Chic
Lemonade Money

De-ann Black

Toffee
Apple

Toffee Apple Publishing

Other books in the Sewing, Knitting & Baking book series are:

Book 1 - The Tea Shop.
Book 2 - The Sewing Bee & Afternoon Tea.
Book 3 - The Christmas Knitting Bee.
Book 4 – Champagne Chic Lemonade Money.
Book 5 – The Vintage Sewing & Knitting Bee.

First published 2014

Published by Toffee Apple Publishing 2018

Champagne Chic Lemonade Money

ISBN: 9781976998768

Toffee
Apple

Toffee Apple Publishing

Also by De-ann Black (Romance, Action/Thrillers & Children's books). See her Amazon Author page or website for further details about her books, screenplays, illustrations, art and fabric designs.
www.De-annBlack.com

Romance:

The Sewing Shop
Heather Park
The Tea Shop by the Sea
The Bookshop by the Seaside
The Sewing Bee
The Quilting Bee
Snow Bells Wedding
Snow Bells Christmas
Summer Sewing Bee
The Chocolatier's Cottage
Christmas Cake Chateau
The Beemaster's Cottage
The Sewing Bee By The Sea
The Flower Hunter's Cottage

The Christmas Knitting Bee
The Sewing Bee & Afternoon Tea
The Vintage Sewing & Knitting Bee
Shed In The City
The Bakery By The Seaside
Champagne Chic Lemonade Money
The Christmas Chocolatier
The Christmas Tea Shop & Bakery
The Vintage Tea Dress Shop In Summer
Oops! I'm The Paparazzi
The Bitch-Proof Suit

Action/Thrillers:

Love Him Forever.
Someone Worse.
Electric Shadows.

The Strife Of Riley.
Shadows Of Murder.

Children's books:

Faeriefied.
Secondhand Spooks.
Poison-Wynd.

Wormhole Wynd.
Science Fashion.
School For Aliens.

Colouring books:

Summer Garden. Spring Garden. Autumn Garden. Sea Dream.
Festive Christmas. Christmas Garden. Flower Bee. Wild Garden.
Faerie Garden Spring. Flower Hunter. Stargazer Space. Bee Garden.

Embroidery books:

Floral Nature Embroidery Designs
Scottish Garden Embroidery Designs

Contents

Chapter One

The Vintage Dressmaker's Shop

The first time I saw him he was walking along the city street on a scorching hot summer morning. He walked right past the shop window where I was working. He wasn't dressed for the July weather. I felt hot just looking at him in his high neck, long sleeve jumper and trousers. A pair of training shoes were the only indication that he was outdoors keeping fit.

And maybe he wasn't.

There was an air of melancholy about him. Everything he wore was black or dark grey, as if he'd tried to make himself a walking shadow. His hair was as dark as his clothes but his face was pale, drawn, a man who'd seen the harsher side of life too often. Despite this, he was handsome, hauntingly so, and I found myself wondering about him long after he'd gone past the shop window.

I estimated he was a few years older than me. A man in his early–mid thirties — tall, fit looking but not in the sense of going to the gym, something else. Something about this man was different and I couldn't fathom what it was.

He hadn't even bothered to glance in the window, though why should he? Vintage dresses and bolts of beautiful fabric wouldn't interest him. Joyce owned the vintage clothes shop and I worked for her as a dressmaker and pattern–maker.

I'd been working since 6:30 a.m. to help get the shop ready for opening at nine.

New stock had arrived the previous afternoon and I'd been busy sifting through it, deciding what pieces I wanted for the window display, and hanging a new painting on the wall.

Joyce, a woman of retirement age, had owned the shop for decades and was an expert dressmaker. The shop was situated in a niche in the centre of Glasgow. Not right in the hub of it, but near enough to enjoy plenty of passing trade. She'd hired me to work for her several months ago along with Alma, another dressmaker around the same age as me. Joyce's shop had become busier as vintage clothing became more popular, and for the first time ever she'd hired staff to help her cope with the increased demand for the lovely

1

clothes she sold — mainly gorgeous dresses, skirts and tops. Anyone looking for a unique dress was sure to find something wonderful hanging in her shop or could request something to be made to order, including wedding dresses and ball gowns.

Joyce and Alma were picking up new fabrics from one of the markets and were due in around 8:30 a.m. They'd also promised to bring back a supply of fresh morning rolls for our breakfast cuppa and cake for the tea break later.

I gazed out the shop window and watched the tall, broad–shouldered figure disappear along the street. Something about him...

I hung the large painting on the wall above the dresser near the counter. It was a retro–style piece I'd painted, a woman's face in bright colours, an eye–catching design. I wanted it to highlight the carousels of sixties, seventies and eighties retro clothing for sale. I loved working for Joyce because she encouraged me to use my artistic skills as well as my sewing and pattern–making.

On the opposite side of the shop hung more traditional vintage clothes — vintage as many of the customers imagined — tea dresses and flowery prints from the 1940s and 1950s, satin gowns from the 1930s and 1920s flapper dresses. Some were original vintage. Others were adapted, upscaled or sewn from scratch using my patterns with suitable fabrics.

The shop offered retro, vintage, second–hand, antique, whatever you wanted to call it. Clothes and accessories from the past available in the present. Preloved and hopefully loved again.

Would I be?

I straightened the painting and tried not to dwell on my disastrous love life. My ex decided he wanted to split up with me in January. I don't know what was the coldest — the wintry weather or the text message from him telling me we were through. He'd found someone else. Someone who didn't fill the house with old–fashioned clothing. Someone who didn't steam the wrinkles out of vintage dresses in the bathroom. Someone who didn't jump up and down when they bought a bargain bundle of linen sheets knowing they'd make loads of dresses and skirts and who couldn't wait to run them up in the sewing machine.

But the heartache had spurred me on. I'd previously worked as a seamstress for a large department store for three years, altering everything from evening dresses to men's shirts. But when I saw an advertisement in Joyce's shop window looking for staff I applied and got the job. Now I could combine my pattern–making skills, dressmaking and art.

Within the shop was a vintage haberdashery which was popular with customers who wanted to sew their own garments. Joyce scoured the markets for inexpensive fabrics, bought them in bulk and passed the savings on to customers. Most of the fabrics were easily affordable, including the linings and notions that were needed for dressmaking and sewing.

Costs were kept to a minimum. Customers could sew their own evening dresses or fabulous tea dresses from the fabrics and patterns we sold. And there was a great selection of vintage items on the rails. Customers soon realised that the bargains enabled them to dress well for less.

I'd been sewing since I was a little girl, and here I was, all these years later, using the same techniques and handy hints I'd learned not only for make do and mend, but to make gorgeous and better. Champagne chic for lemonade money.

I saw Joyce and Alma drive up. They carried in the fabrics they'd bought. I went through to the kitchen at the back of the shop and flicked the kettle on for tea. The premises had previously been a house many years ago and had retained the kitchen and a tiny back garden. There was a bathroom upstairs and two rooms that we used as a stockroom and workroom for sewing new clothes and mending and altering the vintage range.

Jars of beads were kept topped up with everything from colourful seed beads to silver–lined bugle beads that we stitched on to the hemlines of cocktail dresses. We repaired vintage evening dresses and bags that had lost some of their beads, bringing back their shimmer.

Shelves were stacked with fabrics from the past and present — cotton silks, satin, tulle, poplin, linen and chiffon. Threads for machine sewing and embroidery work were kept on thread and bobbin reel spindles, and downstairs they were on display on the hand–painted dressers. Fabrics, knitting yarns and trims galore made the haberdashery a treasure trove for those who loved to sew and knit.

'The window is looking lovely, Bee,' Joyce said to me. No one called me Bedelia.

'I sorted through everything that arrived yesterday.' I pointed to a laundry bag with several items in it. 'Only a handful of the dresses and tops need laundered. The rest are fresh and some have already been cleaned.'

'That'll save us work,' said Joyce. 'Will you be able to photograph them today? We need to update the website.'

'Yes, the light's ideal this morning. Nice and bright. I'll set the camera up and make a start on that now.'

It was part of my job to photograph the clothes once they were ready for sale. Online orders were posted out daily by Alma, and I helped Joyce update the website.

Joyce smiled and held up a large bag of rolls and a cake box. 'The rolls are still warm and I bought a cake for later. Light and delicious.' She went through to the kitchen to make the tea while I set up my camera.

I wondered what type of cake Gilles who owned the coffee shop next door had baked as his speciality of the day. We were forced to taste any new cakes and confections he added to his menu. Gilles' coffee shop had a vintage theme, selling classic cakes and baking. The two shops complemented each other, like a slice of the past in the modern world.

'I bought a coffee and cream sponge,' Joyce called through to me. 'Gilles insisted we try his new recipe.'

'Gilles was very temperamental this morning,' said Alma. She tucked her shiny auburn hair behind her ears and flopped down on one of the chairs behind the counter. Alma was prettier than she gave herself credit for, and her delicate features, large blue eyes and twenties–style bobbed hair were perfect when I needed a model when photographing the cloche hats and fascinators.

'There's a surprise,' I said. Gilles was part French, part Scottish. He was always reminding people that his name was pronounced *gsheel* and that he would only marry a woman who shared his love of vintage and traditional baking and who thought his puff pastry was second to none.

I thought his puff pastry was okay, so I guessed that put me out of the running to marry the much–admired Gilles, though Alma had her eye on him despite denying that she fancied him.

4

Joyce had never married, but she'd been flirting with a tailor in the city who had sold us a supply of herringbone fabric to make a couple of forties–style skirt suits. Since then he'd dropped by several times on any excuse to chat to Joyce including handing in two classic gents coats that he said were surplus to his shop's requirements. We didn't sell a lot of menswear, but Joyce accepted the coats which were snapped up within days of us putting one of them in the front window.

'Raspberry or apricot jam, girls?' Joyce called through to us.

'Apricot,' said Alma.

'Just butter for me.' A tasty buttered roll and a cup of tea was just what I needed. The sun was streaming in the front window, highlighting the summery dresses I'd put on the mannequins. I wore a pastel striped chiffon dress. It was sleeveless and pleated from the collar down to the hem. It fanned out when I walked and the knee–length styling made it a perfect summer dress.

We sat down together at the counter to enjoy our rolls and tea. Joyce was taller than us and very trim with great posture. She wore a skirt and blouse and her light brown, silver–threaded hair was pinned up in a chignon. She tended to wear classic separates which suited her build. I didn't have a particular look. I liked to wear lots of different eras from the twenties to the eighties. Alma loved the forties and fifties even though I often made her pose as a twenties girl. I'd never seen her wear anything from the sixties or psychedelic since I'd met her.

'Your dress matches your painting,' Alma commented to me.

I'd just bitten into a soft, buttery roll and merely nodded. I did match it, though the colours in the painting were a trifle more vibrant.

Joyce took a sip of her tea and sat back in her chair to admire the canvas. 'I really like that painting of yours. It would make a great dress. In fact, I was going to talk to you about something. Could you paint little yachts, a ship's wheel and waves in red, white and two shades of blue? And bunting and bicycles.'

'Erm, yes...' I said. 'What do you want them for?'

'We're diversifying. Having our own fabrics printed. That's why I wanted the cake to celebrate.'

Alma gasped. 'Really?'

Joyce nodded. 'All we have to do is provide the designs and email them off to a company and they'll print them on to various fabrics. They've offered me an amazing deal if I buy in bulk, so everything sort of depends on your artwork, Bee. You'll receive a share of the profits of course.'

'Our own fabrics? With my designs?'

Joyce grinned and adjusted her spectacles. 'Exciting, isn't it?'

I smiled back at her. 'That would be great.' My mind immediately began whirring with lots of ideas.

'And that painting of yours,' Joyce added. 'The one you put up this morning. I'd like to have the design printed on fabric so that customers can make it into a dress. It would work well with your classic shift dress pattern or the wrapover tea dress.'

'Put me down for the first two metres,' said Alma. 'I'd wear that. I love the colours and design. I'll make a little shift dress.'

So before we'd even designed any prints, we'd all earmarked a few metres each of the fabric. And perhaps I'd see Alma wear a retro print dress after all.

The morning wore on. I photographed the new stock and we were kept busy with our sewing and serving customers. Whenever we changed the window display it always attracted customers to come in and browse and buy.

After customers left, Joyce held up a gold sequin evening top. 'Do you have anything at home that would go with this?' she asked me.

'I'll have a look through my wardrobes when I get home.' I was sure I had a long, black fishtail skirt that would go well with it.

Joyce and Alma tried not to giggle and exchanged a girlish look.

'What?'

'Nothing.' Joyce hung the top up on a rail.

Alma kept her lips buttoned and continued to sew the vintage collar accessory she was top stitching on the sewing machine behind the counter.

'What?' I insisted. 'Say it before you burst a seam trying not to laugh.'

Alma let Joyce explain.

'It's just that...your wardrobes...'

'They're not excessive,' I protested.

They both looked at me.

'I only have four wardrobes,' I said. 'Two in the bedroom which isn't excessive considering I don't have much else except a bed in there. And one in the spare room.'

Joyce held up four fingers.

'Okay, so I have one in the living room, but it suits the decor.'

Joyce smiled. 'And a sewing machine, overlocker, cutting table, artwork drawing table and an easel.'

'And a dressmaking mannequin,' Alma chimed–in.

I shrugged. 'I'm a dressmaker.'

'I love your house,' said Alma. 'If I wasn't sharing a flat I'd have my sewing machine in the living room and all the things that you have.'

I lived in a rented house on the outskirts of the city and drove into work each day. Although the shop was closed on Sundays, we tended to work almost every day. If a dress needed mended and it was time to shut up the shop, I'd often work late in the workroom upstairs, or take the dress home with me and finish it, then bring it in the next morning. Joyce paid well and I earned more money working for her than in my previous job. I was now also hopeful of earning a little extra from the fabrics and couldn't wait to start designing them.

During the next two weeks I worked on the designs for the fabrics, painting everything from vintage sewing machines and flowers to dancing people abstracts and traditional teacups to use for the designs. The retro painting design was already away to the printers and was due to arrive soon.

I was in the shop window, putting a summery dress on one of the mannequins, when he walked past. I stared at him but he didn't even notice me. This was the closest I'd been to him. His eyes were green. I was sure of it. They were the only colourful thing about him.

As always, he wore black and grey, a shadow. The day was a scorcher and yet again he wore a high neck top. I felt myself melting in the heat from the sun shining through the front window. I wore a cotton dress. How he could breathe in this summer weather when he was dressed for a cold autumn day?

He walked faster than before. I stood so still he probably mistook me for a mannequin. I pressed my nose against the window to see where he went, but he became lost in the crowd of city shoppers.

Alma wrapped up a dress order ready for posting. 'Was that *him*?'

'Yes,' I said wistfully. I'd mentioned him to them in recent weeks.

Joyce sat at the sewing machine beside the counter making a vintage prom dress for a fifties–style party order. 'I see what you mean by his clothes. Doesn't he feel the heat?'

'Bee certainly does when she looks at him,' Alma teased me.

I threw her a glance. 'I'm just curious.'

'He's very handsome in a harsh sort of way,' said Joyce. 'Very manly.'

Alma stuck the address label on the parcel. 'What do you think he does for a living?'

Joyce fed the dress fabric through the machine. 'He's got money, that's for sure.'

We both looked at Joyce. She could sum someone up from the clothes they wore. We jokingly called her a fashion profiler. I'd never known her to be wrong, so I was keen to hear her assessment of him.

Joyce continued to sew as she created a profile on our mystery man. 'I always look at a man's shoes first.'

'He wore trainers,' I blurted out. Surely she couldn't tell his position in life from training shoes. Brogues, loafers, polished, down–at–heel — I understood that you could tell certain aspects about a man from his shoes, but not trainers.

'Black trainers.' Joyce's tone was clipped, decisive, as if this had told her lots of things that I hadn't even thought of. 'Even the laces were black. Most training shoes, the ones that people wear to go by our window at least, are white or light–coloured with the brand obvious. But his shoes...' she shook her head. 'Trainers. Just black trainers. And not particularly worn. Not new, they've been used, but he either hasn't had those shoes for long or doesn't wear them very often.'

Alma's blue eyes widened. 'What does that mean?'

'I think it means that those shoes are not what he would normally wear. He's wearing them for a specific purpose and when they've served that purpose, he'll go back to his normal life.'

Now it was my turn to gaze wide–eyed at Joyce. My eyes were grey, no match for Alma's in vibrancy, but my dark lashes helped emphasise their upturned corners, as if I was permanently curious about everything. I brushed the strands of blonde hair away from my face. The heat had made my up–do spiral in wispy tendrils around my pale features. Despite loving the sunny weather, my complexion tended to remain pale gold because I lived mainly indoors, peering out at the world during the day through the shop window. I kept meaning to get outdoors and build up my slender frame, but I was always too busy sewing and pattern–making. So pale I remained. I did like to run but I hardly had time for that either.

'What else?' I asked Joyce.

'His hair is very well–cut. A classic cut. And his posture gives him a military bearing.'

'You think he's a Forces man?' I said.

Joyce was thoughtful. 'No, but...he belongs to something that requires him to look extremely well–groomed without any hint of fashion or flair. This man doesn't want, doesn't need or isn't allowed to stand out from the crowd.'

'Is that why he wears clothes that are hard to define?' I said. 'There's nothing from any era, designer or shop that I can pinpoint.'

Joyce nodded at me. 'I think so.'

Before we could delve further into his profile, Gilles came in carrying a tray of fairy cakes. The icing was white and pink and he'd piped cream around the edges.

'Taste these,' he said, thrusting the tray at me. 'I've added pink champagne to the recipe. Give me an honest opinion. Does it make the cakes sparkle with extra flavour?'

I'd learned that it was easier to taste whatever cake Gilles thrust at me without flinching at his forthright manner. There were worse things than having a very attractive man plying you with cake.

'Well, what do you think?' he said, barely giving me time to savour it.

I nodded and gave it the thumbs up.

Joyce helped herself to one. She tasted it and swooned. 'This is delicious.'

Alma bit into one. 'It tastes of vanilla, sweet icing and...'

'Pink champagne?' he prompted her.

She smiled and nodded.

His dark brown eyes relaxed their steely glare. 'I'm including them in a special vintage coffee afternoon promotion. Coffee, cake and a glass of pink champagne.'

'I'm sure your customers will love it,' said Joyce.

He suddenly realised he'd barged straight in, interrupting our conversation. 'I hope I didn't interrupt anything,' he said.

'No,' said Joyce. 'We were just talking about Bee's mystery man.'

The brown eyes flicked to me. 'I didn't know that you were dating anyone.'

'I'm not. He's just a man who walks past the shop window.'

His interest notched up a level. 'And you like this man?'

'I'm just curious about him.'

'He wears dark clothing and has an air of mystery surrounding him,' said Alma. 'And his clothes are far too warm for the summer.'

'And you're all intrigued?'

'It's just women's gossip,' I said.

'Do you gossip about me?' He sounded hopeful.

'Oh yes. You're a hot topic in this shop.' I glanced at Alma but he didn't take the bait.

'And how do I rate in comparison to your mystery man?'

'You both score a ten,' said Alma.

'I have competition then,' he joked. 'I must keep a lookout for this man. What did you say he looked like?'

I described him in detail. With a few tweaks, he was similar to Gilles. Both were tall with short dark hair and in their thirties. Gilles carried a bit more weight, but running his coffee shop kept him active and his arms were strong from all the baking he did. Kneading dough, whipping buttercream into submission and loading trays full of cakes, scones, cottage loaves and buns into the ovens worked those muscles of his which were often on show because of the fitting T–shirts he wore.

Gilles nodded, taking in everything. 'Does he know he's being studied?'

'No,' I said. 'He never looks in.'

'Then he's a fool,' said Gilles, 'because there are three beautiful women in this shop.'

I thought Alma was going to burst with glee. Gilles thought she was beautiful. Even if he had a tendency to ply us with flattery as well as cakes, it was nice to be complimented.

Gilles breezed out, promising to find out about this man whoever he was.

Chapter Two

Champagne Chic

I pinned a metre of fabric on to one of the mannequins in the window display. Our new fabrics were starting to sell well and I'd designed other prints that were suitable for the autumn. The hot summer had mellowed to become a lovely deep autumn in the city.

I draped the fabric around the mannequin to make it look like a tea dress. It was a floral print in rich gold, bronze and autumnal shades. I adjusted the little spotlights in the window and hoped that the early evening glow from the burnished sky would add the right amount of light for the photographs. Whenever a new fabric was delivered, I tried to photograph it on a mannequin so that customers viewing it on the website could see how it would look when made up.

I set my camera up and began taking snaps. From glancing at the previews, the fabric was going to look great.

The busy day was winding down, people were heading home and the light was fading fast. I went outside to see if I could capture a few snaps of the makeshift dress through the window.

For a moment I thought I saw him. I hadn't seen him for a few weeks. I blinked, but the figure had disappeared into the crowd. It probably wasn't him I decided, just a trick of the light or my imagination. I'd been thinking about him. I didn't know why. I guess I wondered what had happened to him. I'd almost become accustomed to him going past.

Gilles waved to me from the coffee shop window. Whenever he saw me with my camera he'd ask me to photograph his latest cakes for him. I didn't mind, especially as he was rubbish at photography and gave us cakes in exchange for the pictures. He used them on his website, and we also used his coffee shop as a backdrop for a few of our vintage dress photographs.

'Could you photograph the mocha cake and fruit muffins?' he said as I stepped inside his shop. I loved the atmosphere, the old–fashioned tables and chairs, the vintage decor in creams and various shades of coffee along with the dark wood flooring and oak beams. His customers came to enjoy the experience of the place as well as the baking and wonderful selection of coffee. A set of old brass scales, polished to perfection, were used to weigh the coffee beans. Mismatched china was used to serve the beverages and cakes, and every coffee pot was an individual vintage original that customers treated with as much care as Gilles did. He had two members of staff, but it was Gilles who was often behind the counter, chatting to customers and advising them on their coffee selection to go with whatever they'd chosen from the patisserie.

The subtle lighting always made me feel as if I'd stepped back into another era, to a time that felt cosy and comforting.

I set up the cake and muffins on a table near the window. I smoothed the linen tablecloth, added a floral coffee pot, a bowl of crystallised brown sugar, cream jug and other little bits and pieces to create an appetising and attractive setting.

Despite being a fusspot about his cakes and coffee, Gilles never interfered when I set things up to take the photographs. But he watched, fascinated and delighted.

I snapped numerous shots, ensuring I'd captured the delicious texture of his mouth–watering mocha cake. My tummy rumbled. I'd had a hectic day. Lunch was a sandwich that I hadn't even finished. We'd been extra busy with customers' orders for everything from cocktail dresses to velvet capes. I'd skipped breakfast because I was running late and was now ticking over on the remnants of a salad sandwich and numerous cups of tea. I planned to make a hearty dinner when I got home, but the reality was more likely to be something zapped in the microwave before I flopped down on the sofa.

'I'll email the photos to you later tonight,' I promised Gilles.

'Thanks, Bee. I appreciate it.' He glanced at my hair. 'Busy day?'

I smoothed the tendrils back from my face. 'Oh yes.'

'You still look lovely.'

Smooth as ever. Unlike my hair which had started the day as a chic chignon and was now more wild woman or thrown through a hedge backwards. Probably the latter. I hadn't been remotely wild in a long time. Chance would be a fine thing, especially when it came to meeting someone I wanted to date. Working for Joyce was fun but I quickly realised that most of our customers were women. Men were more inclined to be reluctant shoppers, dragged in by their wives or girlfriends. Trawling through the rails of clothes could take ages, especially as ladies were encouraged to try items on before buying because sizes varied depending on the era. It was far better to try a dress on before purchasing. So the men tended to slope off next door to the coffee shop. I was sure Gilles' business benefited enormously from this surplus trade, though to be fair, we also gained customers who popped into his shop for coffee and cake and saw the array of lovely vintage wear in our shop window.

Work swallowed up most of my life and there were hardly any pockets of time when I had the chance to meet someone wonderful. Christmas was on the far horizon. Party season. Joyce said the shop was at its busiest during the holidays. Party invites were part of the fashion frenzy when customers would snap up the perfect glittering party dress for a minimum cost. That was when the shop's champagne chic really sparkled for lemonade money. Bargains galore were on offer — and lots of party invitations.

This would be my first Christmas working at the shop, and Alma's. I was looking forward to it. And maybe I'd bag a man for Christmas this year, or at least find someone to kiss under the mistletoe. My ex despised Christmas. Now I was free to enjoy every sparkly, tinsel–filled moment. Christmas in Glasgow was great. There were loads of shows, the shop windows were all done up and the Christmas light displays were dazzling. Of course, it was still autumn, but the summer had chomped in and suddenly I was wearing a cardigan along with my classic polka dot 50s dress with its sweetheart neckline.

I was just about to click my camera off when I saw *him* running along the street. From the coffee shop window I could see him approaching from a distance. Without thinking how Gilles would react I pointed towards the advancing figure. 'There he is. That's him.'

Gilles ran to the door and looked up the street. 'The man with the dark hair and dark T–shirt?'

'Yes,' I whispered, as if he could hear me from this distance, though he was running, not fast, but fast enough to be closing the gap. Within moments he would be right outside the coffee shop.

I had the camera in my hands. Gilles grabbed it. 'I'll get a picture of him.' He hurried outside.

I hurried after him. 'No, don't do that. He could say something. He'll think we're weird.'

Gilles paid no heed to my protests and fiddled with the buttons on the camera which sent me into overdrive.

'Don't touch the settings,' I shrieked at him. 'You'll delete all the images.' I lunged at Gilles, more concerned about saving my work, including the pictures I'd taken earlier in the day of the new sixties dresses that had arrived as well as the mannequin shots, than causing a scene or bothering about *him*.

Determined to keep control of the camera, and tall and strong enough to thwart my efforts, Gilles continued to press the buttons and adjust the camera so that he could snap the stranger who by now was within spitting distance.

What happened next was a bit of a blur. I was wrestling the camera from Gilles and shouting, 'Let go of my camera. Don't touch it. Give me my camera back now.' Or words to that effect. There was probably an expletive thrown in.

The next thing I knew, Gilles' arm was twisted up his back. 'Give the lady her camera back,' the man said in a voice that was deep and determined.

Gilles hesitated for a second, so pressure was put on his arm, causing him to wince from the pain, and the man repeated the order, this time with more threat in his tone.

Gilles handed the camera to the man, who then threw him aside as if he was a sweetie wrapper. Gilles tumbled into the doorway of the coffee shop.

The intense green eyes gazed down at me. Wow! He. Was. Gorgeous.

He handed me the camera.

I accepted it.

Not a word was exchanged.

I blinked, and he continued running along the street.

What the hell just happened?

Gilles was shaken and a little bit stirred. I ushered him inside and poured him a coffee.

'What the hell just happened?' he gasped.

'My thoughts entirely.'

'He obviously thought I was trying to steal your camera.'

'It's your own fault. You should've given it back to me when I told you to.'

Gilles rubbed the top of his arm and rolled his shoulder to see if any damage had been done. No damage, except to his ego.

'He must do some sort of stuff,' Gilles complained.

Luckily there were no customers around to see him get a mild hiding. The coffee shop was about to close for the night and the two staff were through in the kitchen clearing up. They'd missed the drama, though I was sure Gilles would relay every detail.

'What do you mean, stuff?'

Gilles waved his arms around in mock fighting postures. 'Martial arts stuff. I didn't have a chance. He grabbed me in a grip of steel.'

Now it was Gilles' turn to throw a few expletives into the ring.

I let him get his wind out, though in the back of my mind I couldn't wait to tell Joyce. Another snippet of information for her to add to his profile.

'I used to date a man who did jiu–jitsu,' Joyce confided.

We'd closed the shop for the night and the three of us sat huddled drinking tea and pouring over the details of the fracas.

Alma broke open a packet of chocolate digestives and we nibbled on those while Joyce assessed the latest information.

'He was a right soor dook,' Joyce reminisced, 'but oh he was handsome. I used to kid myself on that I could soften his hard–as–bone nature. Deep down I knew we'd never last and I really just fancied the pants off him. Anyway...no one, including me, knew that he was an expert in jiu–jitsu and had trained since he was a wee boy. We only found out when two men got on his bad side and he hammered them into the floorboards so fast that we hardly knew what had happened. We split up not long after that.'

I sipped my tea. 'So you think he maybe does jiu–jitsu?'

'He certainly knew how to handle Gilles.'

Alma brushed biscuit crumbs off her nice boucle skirt. 'Gilles is no pushover either. I've seen him chuck troublesome customers out of his coffee shop without breaking a sweat. He threw two out into the street during the summer. I think the heat had got their hackles up. They were fighting each other over the last frangipane slice at the patisserie counter and putting customers off their coffee. Gilles grabbed them both at the same time and threw them outside. They put up quite a struggle but neither of the women were a match for Gilles. I could see the muscles on his biceps straining as he had one of them by the scruff of the neck and the other in an arm lock. I like a man with muscles,' she added wistfully.

'What we need is more information,' said Joyce. 'He's never going to come into the shop, so you'll have to follow him the next time you see him and find out where he lives.'

I'd been tempted to follow him just to see where he went, so although Joyce's suggestion gave me the wobbles, I was sort of up for it. 'He could live miles from here on the outskirts of the city.'

Joyce shook her head. 'No, he lives in the city centre. No one who lived outside the city would come here to keep fit. They'd run along the streets where it was quieter. Nope, he lives or works near here.'

Okay, this made sense. But to follow him? I wasn't sure. 'What if he sees me?'

Joyce shrugged. 'It's a big city. It's far easier to follow someone in a crowd.'

Alma's blue eyes twinkled and then she said, 'I'll ask him who he is and what he does.'

'No, Alma, no,' I said.

Joyce agreed. 'You can't walk right up to him and ask him that.'

Alma was adamant. 'Yes I can. I'll ask him what his name is and what he does for a living. Men aren't complicated. He'll tell me.'

'He'll think you're crazy,' I said.

'But he'll still tell me. Men always tell me what I want.'

'No,' said Joyce. 'Let Bee follow him first. If that doesn't work, then you can brazen it out with him.'

So that was the plan.

We finished our tea and I checked that my photographs hadn't been deleted while Joyce flicked the lights off and locked up the shop. She kept the spotlights on in the window.

I clicked the preview button. And there he was. The last picture that the camera had taken was always the first to show on the little preview screen. 'I've got a picture of him,' I shrieked. 'Look. There he is. Gilles must've taken a photograph of him when he was fiddling with the buttons.'

By the glow of the window lights we peered at his face. Such a handsome face. And his eyes were definitely green. Like green ice. Clear and cool — and sexy.

'Wow!' said Alma. 'He's gorgeous in close–up.'

'A handsome–looking man.' Joyce adjusted her spectacles. 'Enlarge the image, Bee. He's got fine, silvery scars on his upper cheekbones.' She nodded thoughtfully. 'Yes, this man has seen many a fight. But he's not a boxer. His nose hasn't been broken or any other bones in his face, and he doesn't have a boxer's posture.'

Now I was even more intrigued. So fascinated and attracted to him that I almost considered encouraging Alma to ask him outright. Then I thought, no, I'd do what Joyce suggested. The next time he went past the shop I would follow him to see where he went.

It was two weeks before I saw him again, and of course, it had to be raining. Not pouring, but that smirry rain that casts everything in soft focus.

'There he is.' I didn't even need to elaborate.

'Action stations,' shouted Joyce, thrusting her large vintage floral umbrella at me.

'It's raining,' I said, wondering if my ankle boots would slip in the wet. I was wearing a yellow, skinny rib jumper from the sixties with a hand stitched appliqué on each sleeve, a chocolate brown corduroy pinafore dress that I'd made, ribbed black tights, and my hair was tied back in a ponytail secured with a vintage hair clasp.

'All the better,' said Joyce. 'You can hide behind the umbrella. It's a handy disguise.'

I almost laughed. There was no disguising this umbrella. Frills, brightly coloured flowers printed on it.

He was running along the street and getting closer. There was no time to hesitate.

Alma peered out the window. 'He's soaking wet. He's just wearing a T–shirt and trousers. Not even a jacket in this weather. And it's been raining all day. He must be hard as nails.'

Why did he over–dress for the summer and wear less for a cold, rainy autumn day? And in the summer he was walking. Now he was running. It was as if his world was complete opposites. I couldn't figure it out.

Joyce grabbed me by the shoulders and pushed me towards the door to launch me the moment he went past. 'Remember, try to keep pace with him, Bee. You can run. You're fast on your feet.'

Shoppers were scurrying for shelter or running to catch a bus, so I supposed I wouldn't look odd running in the rain. It was late afternoon. The day was overcast but there was a cosiness to the city as the streetlamps began to flicker into life and the glow from the shops reflected on the puddles.

I joined the sea of umbrellas and hurried after him. My lungs filled with the cold, damp air, but it livened me up rather than made me shiver. The chase was on.

Chapter Three

Designing Patterns & Dressmaking

He was fast. But I kept up with him. Oh yes I did.

Frilly umbrella and corduroy pinafore aside, I ran like the wind. I loved to run, obviously not along the street on a day like this wearing these boots but at least the heels were flat. A bus driver did me the enormous courtesy of pausing and waving at me to jump on board thinking I was a passenger and not the woman wearing vintage chasing after the man dressed in black.

Spurred on by the refreshing atmosphere and the sheer sense of mischief, I bolted after him, ducking and diving past other shoppers wielding umbrellas. No one batted an eyelid. They were all too busy going about their own business to bother about me.

I raced along the street following a short distance after the tall, shadowy figure. Then he took a sharp detour and I lost him for a moment as the traffic split us up. I darted across the road and put a spurt on to close the gap. If he kept running in squares I'd have to give up. I was fit but not that fit. I'd soon be out of steam and would have to let him go.

Then I lost him in the crowd when a delivery van got in my way, obscuring my view. Had he gone left or right? Had he double–backed? Where the hell was this man running to? I stopped and looked around me. Damn. He'd gone.

I trudged back along the street and had only walked past a couple of shops when a voice called out to me from a sheltered doorway.

'You're not very adept at this, are you?'

Droplets of water whirled off my umbrella as I spun around to see him standing there looking at me. The green eyes blinked away the rain, clear and defiant.

I could've pretended that I didn't know he was talking to me, or that he knew I was following him, but I sensed I'd be wasting my time. We both knew what I'd been up to. There was no point in lying.

'I haven't had a lot of practise. And I'm wearing my slippy boots.'

The firm lips curved into a wry smile. I'd amused him, or was he laughing at my effort to brazen it out.

He stepped out from the doorway into the drizzling rain. His black T–shirt clung to every lean–muscled contour of his broad shoulders, lithe arms and slim–hipped physique. The fabric accentuated the taut abdominals that were in evidence as he moved towards me, as did his dark trousers that emphasised his long legs. The rain shimmered like liquid crystal on his handsome face and dripped sexily off the tips of his short dark hair.

If ever I was mesmerised...

I'd seen pictures of men like this is adverts, in films, in art, but never for real. He was real, wasn't he? My stomach tightened when I looked at him — trepidation, excitement, lust...

'Go back to the shop.'

I blinked. He knew I worked in the shop? 'You've seen me?' The words were murmured as my thoughts spilled out uncontrollably. 'I didn't think you'd even looked at the shop.'

'I don't look at the shop,' his deep voice corrected me. 'I look at the woman who watches me.'

My stomach flipped. Should I deny it? No. Those eyes could see right through me. Then I remembered what Alma said. *'I'll ask him who he is and what he does.'*

I took a deep breath. The damp air felt both cold and yet invigorating. Come on, I urged myself. Ask him. Do it!

'What's your name?' I clutched tightly to the handle of the umbrella. There. I'd said it. I waited for his response.

He didn't even flinch. His reply was smooth. 'Innes.'

Another deep breath. 'What do you do for a living?'

'I can't tell you that.' No change in his tone. No flicker of reaction on that handsome face of his.

I forced myself not to fidget though my nerves were jangling. 'Why not?' I smiled, feeling a sudden surge of girlish flirtation rising inside me. 'Is it a secret?'

He held my gaze, strong and steady.

I twirled the handle of my umbrella, then stopped and tried to remain calm. 'I mean, what's so secret that you can't tell me?'

Nothing.

'You're not in the Forces, are you?'

One slow shake of his head.

'The Police Force?'

Another calm, silent no.

He wasn't going to tell me, but he obviously wanted me to guess. If I guessed right, would he tell me? And why all the secrecy? Here we were, standing in the rain, with me trying to guess what his job was. I looked at him, and in that moment, just that split second, I saw the melancholy in him. The look that had first caught my interest. Yes, deep inside he wanted me to know and yet...I sensed he wasn't allowed to tell me. So why even entertain this discussion? This game playing. Who worked as something so secret that they couldn't divulge even a slight hint? My mind whirred, flicking as it often did to my favourite films. What hero types were so secret and fit and could fight like the way he'd handled Gilles... And then it hit me. No, he couldn't be. I smiled at the thought of it and spoke without thinking of the consequences if I was right. 'You're not a secret agent are you? Working in some sort of special capacity for the Government and off on top secret missions?' I was still smiling at my silliness as his face gave me his reply.

My heart thudded so hard I was sure he could hear it.

'The rain's getting heavier. Go back to the shop, Bee.' He started to walk away.

'I didn't tell you my name,' I shouted after him.

'Neither you did.'

I tried to fit a small size ten dress on to one of the mannequins in the window. It was a snug fit and I struggled to zip it up the back. I finally managed to zip and fasten it, though it looked fit to burst, rather like me. I'd decided not to tell Joyce or Alma that Innes could be a secret agent to protect him, to protect me, for various reasons, but oh my I was bursting to tell them.

I unzipped the dress and put another one on the mannequin — a floaty chiffon number with layers of frills.

Joyce had closed the shop and was making tea in the kitchen and chatting to Alma while I got the window display ready for the following day. I didn't have to. I could've left it until the morning, but I couldn't sit still and needed something to do until the adrenalin that had been pumping through my system since my encounter with Innes had watered down in potency.

Joyce carried through the tea and biscuits on a tray. Alma scurried after her. She'd been wearing a pair of platform shoes all day trying to see if she could warm to them.

'So his name's Innes?' said Joyce, settling down with a cuppa.

Alma took her shoes off, wiggled her toes, grabbed a shortbread biscuit from the tray along with her tea, and got ready to hear every detail of what had happened.

There was no way I could keep everything quiet. Apart from not being any good at lying to people I liked, Joyce would suss out a fib and would know if I said I'd never spoken to him. So I told them everything except the part about the secret agent.

Alma's eyes widened in their usual curious fashion. 'He knew your name?'

'Yes. He knew I'd been watching him from the shop window. He must've checked the shop's website and seen my name there.' The website had a brief bio about Alma and me as well as featuring Joyce as the owner.

'Well, if he knows your name and what you do, he can ask you out on a date,' said Alma.

'He's not going to ask me out.'

Joyce frowned. 'What's wrong, Bee? You seem so...serious.'

'I'm just shivery with the rain and from having him catch me following him.'

Joyce smiled kindly. 'Drink your tea. That'll warm you up.' She went over to one of the shelves where we kept the shawls and stoles. 'Here, put this around your shoulders.' She draped a cosy woollen shawl around me and gave my shoulders a comforting squeeze. 'Men flip our senses in all sorts of unsettling ways.'

Normally I would've agreed with her. Men I'd fancied before, including my ex, made me giddy at times with excitement, but Innes...not only had he made my senses flip, he'd made my tummy do a triple somersault. I needed to go home and relax on the sofa, snuggle up with a blanket, drink tea, flake out in front of the television and watch a film.

So that's what I did. All was fine until the film finished. A romantic comedy was the perfect tonic. However, the action adventure spy thriller that came on next made me reach for the off button.

I lay in bed wondering if I'd see him again, or if by guessing what he did, he'd disappear from my life. Maybe he'd stop running past the shop and take a different route. Glasgow was a big city.

Thinking I'd never see him again, I drifted off to sleep listening to the rain hitting off the bedroom window. I liked nights like this. Nights when it felt cosy to snuggle under the duvet. I'd pinned twinkle lights around the edges of the window. I'd put them up the day after my ex left me, and vowed never again to become involved with a man who detested Christmas and sneered at the mention of anything sparkly.

I sighed and watched how the lights glittered against the rain pouring down the window. It was just as well that I wasn't going to fall for a secret agent. I couldn't imagine that a man who did daring and dangerous things would appreciate the finer things in life like twinkle lights, silver sprinkles on fairy cakes and sparkly knitted tea cosies.

I was better off forgetting all about him. Tomorrow we were due a delivery of more of our new fabrics. I'd already cut the paper pattern pieces out for a stylish top and tea dress that I was planning to make with them. And I'd recently finished designing a pattern for a classic raincoat, something I'd always wanted to sew. I'd made a toile, a mock–up of the coat, using a plain cream cotton. It was upstairs in the shop, on one of the mannequins in the workroom, and I'd been adjusting the revers and vents on it during lunch breaks and after hours.

I pulled the duvet around me and tried not to think about Innes, but I kept picturing those stunning green eyes of his and the rain running down his handsome face.

The new fabrics lived up to our expectations and I helped Joyce stack them on the haberdashery shelves.

Joyce pointed to two particular rolls of fabric that were on the counter. 'Do you want me to cut the fabric you'll need for your dress and top before we add these for sale?'

'Yes, thanks, Joyce.'

She measured the fabric, cut the amount required, and then I stacked the rolls of cotton silk and soft jersey fabrics on the shelves.

Joyce unpacked the rest of the delivery. 'The cushion cover fabric has arrived as well.'

Alma was busy serving a customer but she perked up when she heard this.

Joyce held up the fabric to show Alma the four designs.

Alma gave us the thumbs up. 'Those are lovely. They'll look very stylish on our display.'

'Could you run these up for us today, Bee?' said Joyce. 'The cushions are upstairs in the stockroom.'

'Yes, I'm keen to see what they look like when they're made up.' I took the fabric upstairs to the workroom, sat down at my sewing machine and made a start on the cushion covers. My sturdy sewing table and chair were beside the window and I had a great view of the city. The streets were busy with people and traffic. I loved the energy that Glasgow had and couldn't imagine living or working anywhere else.

The sky was grey and thunder clouds pressed down upon the city, but I had a sense of excitement. I always enjoyed sewing upstairs above the shop. It felt safe and cosy and I loved the atmosphere and old–fashioned decor that Joyce had refused to modernise. She'd even kept the standard lamp in the corner that the original owners had left along with various other pieces of furniture that we still used. A large vintage rug covered the centre of the floor and the edges had linoleum. The rich colours of the rug brought warmth to the room, as did the lamps with their glass shades.

By the time Joyce called up to me that the kettle was going on for our mid–morning tea, I'd finished the covers and put them on the cushions. Very nice, I thought to myself. Very nice indeed.

I carried the four cushions downstairs and propped them up on the velvet sofa that customers liked to lounge on.

Joyce stood back to admire them. 'Those look brilliant.'

Alma brought the tray of tea and shortbread through. We sat down for our daily chat and cuppa. I glanced out the window. Pouring rain sent shoppers scurrying for shelter.

'I've ordered our Christmas fabrics,' said Joyce.

Alma spluttered into her tea. 'Christmas?'

'It'll be the first day of winter soon,' Joyce told her.

Alma pulled her cardigan around her. 'It has been getting colder in the mornings.'

'There's always a cheery atmosphere in the shop in the winter,' said Joyce. 'Busy but cheery.'

25

'Talking about me?' a man said.

'No, Gilles,' said Joyce, 'just about the shop. I was telling the girls how busy it gets at Christmas time.'

'I thought you ladies would be chatting about the latest gossip.'

'What gossip would that be?' Alma asked him.

'About Bee chasing after that man in the pouring rain.'

'Who told you about that?' I said.

'Oh, a few people. You didn't exactly blend into the crowd, Bee, not with that umbrella.'

'What else did they say about me?'

He tried to sound nonchalant. 'Nothing much, except that when you caught up with him you snogged him in a shop doorway before running away again.'

'I did not.'

He shrugged. 'Just relaying the gossip, Bee.'

Joyce and Alma glared at me.

'You snogged him?' said Alma.

'No, I didn't.'

Joyce studied me. 'Did something else happen that you're not telling us?'

'No,' I fibbed. 'And I definitely did not kiss him or anything like that. I spoke to him for a couple of minutes and then I headed back to the shop.'

Joyce looked at me over the rim of her spectacles.

'I didn't kiss Innes,' I insisted.

She saw that I was telling the truth and turned on Gilles. 'Tell whoever is passing on the gossip that they're talking shite.'

'I'm just relaying what's buzzing along the grapevine,' he said.

'Well you can buzz off back to your shop, Gilles,' Joyce told him.

'Something happened or you wouldn't be so touchy about it,' he said, and headed out. 'I like your new cushions,' he called to us over his shoulder.

'Thank you,' Joyce called back to him.

After assuring Joyce and Alma that I hadn't kissed Innes, I went back upstairs to get on with my sewing. There were two new vintage–style tops to be finished.

I thought about Innes while I sewed. I let my thoughts drift and wondered what it would've been like to kiss him. His lips looked so kissable, wet with rain.

'Bee, are you coming down for your lunch?' Alma shouted up to me. 'Joyce is heating our baked potatoes in the microwave.'

I flicked my sewing machine off and went downstairs.

Joyce always closed the shop for lunch, unless we were inundated with customers.

'Baked beans, salad or cheese?' Joyce offered me the options as I went into the kitchen.

'Salad and a spoonful of baked beans please.'

'I'll have the same,' said Alma.

The three of us sat around the little kitchen table eating our baked potatoes. A large pot of tea, kept warm with a knitted tea cosy that Joyce had made, nestled on the wooden dresser where she kept the plates, other crockery and cutlery.

'We sold the two cocktail dresses that arrived a few days ago,' Alma said to me, detailing what had been sold that morning.

'I loved the one with the gold sequins.' I'd been tempted to buy it but I realised I needed to clear out some of the clothes from my numerous wardrobes rather than add more dresses to them.

'Me too,' said Alma. 'That's the problem working here. I want to keep all the gorgeous clothes for myself.'

'I used to be like that,' Joyce admitted. 'Then I decided that I couldn't keep every dress that I wanted. I still sometimes get a bit sad seeing a favourite piece leave the shop when someone buys it.'

'I'm giving that little dress with the pink crystals I bought a couple of months ago an outing tonight,' said Alma. 'Someone's asked me out on a date.'

'Gilles?' I'd seen him talking to her earlier and assumed it was him.

'No, it's someone I've met a few times when I've been out with friends, and he's asked me to go a party with him this evening. He said he's liked me for a while but never had the nerve to ask me out. I was going to say no, then I thought, why not? He's nice. He works in the management side of fashion retail so we've always had things to chat about.'

'What about Gilles?' Joyce asked her. 'I thought you liked him.'

'I do, but he's not interested in me. He fancies Bee.'

27

I looked at her.

'It's true, and you're the only woman I know who doesn't fancy him.'

Joyce was thoughtful. 'I've sometimes wondered why you don't give Gilles a bit of encouragement.'

'Yes,' Alma agreed. 'All you need to do is lie and flatter his puff pastry and you're in.'

I laughed.

'Maybe it was bad timing when you first met him,' Joyce suggested. 'You'd recently split up with your boyfriend and perhaps you weren't ready to jump into another relationship. And now you've become accustomed to thinking you don't fancy Gilles.'

I sighed and sipped my tea. I had to admit they did have a point.

'Gilles is handsome and a hard working businessman.' Joyce's sales pitch made me wonder if they were right.

Joyce then went for the hard sell. 'I know you like Innes, but that man is a shadow in the wind. You said that he's not going to ask you out, so be careful not to get carried away with the thought of him. A man who breezes in and out of your life isn't going to keep you warm on a cold winter's night.'

I started to clear our plates away and ran the water in the sink. 'I'll think about it, okay?'

'Seriously, Bee, you should give Gilles a second thought,' said Alma. 'He could be the man for you.'

Chapter Four

Coffee Shop & Vintage Fashion

For the next few weeks I reconsidered my feelings about Gilles, long enough for the last leaves of autumn to be swept away by the brisk chill of winter.

I was wrapped up in a vintage coat with a velvet collar turned up against the cold. I'd parked my car further along the street and hurried towards the shop. Joyce and Alma were off to the early morning market and I had the keys to open up the shop.

At 7:30 a.m. on a dark wintry morning, the street was fairly quiet. Only a handful of people were scurrying along heading to work, so the solitary figure of a man at the far end of the street stood out.

Innes?

The wind was so cold it made my eyes sting and I blinked to see if it was him. The man wore a classic dark wool coat. His hands were thrust into the pockets as if he'd been standing there for a while waiting on someone. Waiting on me?

I blinked again and he started to walk away.

'I saw Innes this morning,' I told Joyce and Alma when they arrived with the trims and treasures they'd bought at the market.

Alma looked the most disappointed. Her first date with her new boyfriend had expanded into dating him on a regular basis. When a vintage hat that had been worn to fancy garden parties arrived as part of a collection of stock, Joyce joked that she was putting it aside to wear to Alma's wedding in the near future.

'Don't go daydreaming over Innes again, Bee,' Alma advised me. She glanced at Joyce. 'Should we tell her?'

'Tell me what?'

'We were hoping to keep it as a surprise,' Joyce explained. 'Gilles is planning a party in his coffee shop tomorrow night. It's to celebrate his new winter menu. You know what he's like for promoting his cakes. Well, he confided in us that he's going to ask you out, once he's plied us all with cake, coffee and champagne. We promised him we wouldn't tell you. He wants to surprise you.'

I sat down on the chair beside the sewing machine. 'You've all surprised me.'

Alma leaned down and put her hand on my shoulder. 'So you see, you can't start thinking about Innes again, not when Gilles is going to ask you out to dinner.'

Joyce looked at me. 'Give Gilles a chance.'

Alma agreed. 'At least snog him.'

I laughed.

Alma was adamant. 'Really, Bee. If you snog Gilles you'll soon know if there's any spark of passion between you.' She smiled at me. 'There are worse things than kissing a handsome man who bakes great cakes.'

And so I agreed to be surprised when Gilles put his plan into action.

Joyce locked up the shop and the three of us hurried next door to the coffee shop. It was raining but we were all dressed up to party. Although we hadn't intended to outshine everyone else, our beaded and sequin dresses had more sparkle than the glasses of champagne that were being poured for the other invited guests. Joyce wore a dark blue silk dress that was embellished with beadwork. Alma looked lovely in a sparkly little repro dress that Joyce had made from one of my patterns. The sequins glittered under the lights, as did the sequins on my cocktail dress.

'What will happen if I do have dinner with Gilles and then things don't work out?' I whispered to Joyce. 'It'll be awkward.'

Joyce brushed my concerns aside. 'Nonsense. If it all goes pear–shaped, I'll tell Gilles to suck it up and then we'll all enjoy eating cake and be friends again.'

Fair enough, I thought.

The coffee shop was busy and there was a great party atmosphere. Everyone was well–dressed including Gilles who wore a white shirt and silk tie rather than his usual tight–fitting T–shirts. There was no disguising his muscular physique. Even with his shirt on it was obvious that Gilles was fit and strong. He smiled when he saw me and my heart lifted a little. Could I find happiness with Gilles? Could I?

Gilles hurried over when he saw us arrive. He kissed my hand. 'You look beautiful, Bee.'

I smiled at him.

'You all look beautiful,' he added. 'Come in and enjoy a taste of my new cake selection. I've baked it specially for the winter season. Let me know what you think.'

Joyce and Alma were handed glasses of champagne and taken over to the patisserie where a delicious selection of cakes were displayed on vintage stands.

Gilles kept a hold of my hand and led me to the back of the shop. 'I wanted to ask you something,' he said so that no one else could hear.

I looked up at him.

'You know I've liked you for a long time, Bee. Have dinner with me tomorrow night.'

Although I knew he was going to ask me, I didn't need to feign surprise. Seeing him gaze at me really did take me off guard.

I hesitated.

'Just dinner, Bee.'

'Okay.'

Gilles smiled which made me smile too. I almost wished he'd sweep me off to dinner there and then rather than have to wait. I wanted to know if we'd hit it off. What if Joyce and Alma were right? What if Gilles was the man for me?

'Wherever did you get that dress?' a woman asked me while Gilles attended to his guests.

I told her about Joyce's shop. 'This is a repro vintage that I made myself. We make vintage–style clothes as well as sell originals.'

'I'll have to pop in and browse,' the woman said.

'Do you sell fabric?' another woman asked, overhearing our conversation.

'Yes, we've got a lovely selection of fabrics and a vintage haberdashery stocked with ribbons, trims and yarn.'

'Oh I love to sew and knit,' she said. 'Are you open tomorrow?'

'Yes we are. We open at nine in the morning and close around five.'

'Perfect. If I bring a dress pattern along, could you advise me on what fabrics would be suitable?'

'I certainly will,' I said. 'And we also offer to help existing customers with alterations if they get stuck with tricky parts of their dress patterns.'

'I must tell the girls about this,' the first woman said. 'I'd quite like to get back into my sewing, but I'm never sure about buying fabrics especially knit fabrics that are stretchy.'

'We'd be happy to help you,' I told her.

Gilles approached us. 'I'm stealing Bee away, ladies. I want to tempt her with my sugar buns.'

'Some women have all the luck,' one of the women said.

I heard them giggling as Gilles led me over to the cake display.

I'd been allowing Gilles to tempt me with the new cakes on his winter menu when Joyce came over to me.

'Bee, a few women have been asking if I'll open up the shop to let them buy the dresses in the window display. They've also been admiring our dresses and want to browse through the rails. Alma's coming with me to help. I wanted to let you know where we'd gone.'

'I'll come and help too,' I said, suddenly feeling overwhelmed by Gilles' attention. I needed some fresh air. I smiled at Gilles who seemed to understand that sometimes business had to be attended to. Besides, I'd already agreed to have dinner with him.

The rain had stopped but the street was glistening wet and the air was icy cold. Despite this, several women from the party followed us into Joyce's shop. They were chattering and excited about having a look through all the clothes and fabrics and were as bubbly as the champagne they'd been drinking.

For the next hour or so the party expanded to include both shops and at one point I heard Gilles explain that it was all part of his promotion when he popped in to deposit two women who were keen to see the dresses.

We were rushed off our feet serving customers, explaining about how to make the vintage dresses work for them, and advising on fabrics and accessories. The shop was jumping with energy and laughter and the happy atmosphere made it feel as if we were still partying.

The shop had two changing rooms which were continually busy so most of the women were using the shop as a communal changing area and trying the clothes on where they stood which brought even more squeals of mischief. Despite the shop being lit up like a beacon and passers by being able to peer in the window, the ladies threw decorum to the wind and had their undies on show while they ran around giggling and looking for another dress in their size.

We sold dresses, skirts, tops and fascinators as well as accessories such as the gorgeous hair combs that sparkled with diamante. Strands of lustrous pearls were snapped up, especially the long strands that worked so well with the vintage fashion dresses.

Alma ran up the stairs to the storeroom to bring down other items for customers to try on, while Joyce measured and cut numerous pieces of fabric at the haberdashery counter.

A woman wearing only her bra and panties held up a dress to me. 'This says it's my size but it's too small. Do the vintage sizes differ from modern sizes?'

'Some of the vintage dresses vary in comparison to women's sizes nowadays. We advise all our customers to try things on. However, our own range of new vintage–style dresses, skirts and tops are based on modern sizing.' I helped her choose four dresses that I thought would be a better fit and would flatter her figure shape.

'Can I run next door to the coffee shop to show my husband this dress?' a customer asked Joyce. She wore a shimmering crystal encrusted evening dress that she was eager to buy. 'I'll make sure to hold up the hem so it doesn't touch the ground,' she promised.

'Yes,' said Joyce. 'I hope he likes it.'

And off she went, running into Gilles' shop. This led to other women asking permission to do the same, so now there was a stream of ladies wearing vintage chic gallivanting from one shop to the other.

Joyce finally closed the shop as the party came to an end around midnight. She turned the overhead lights off leaving the table lamps on to give the shop a warm glow. Alma stacked the rolls of fabric on to the shelves and tidied the haberdashery.

'We've sold a ton of things,' said Joyce. She glanced at the mannequins in the window. 'Not a stitch left on any of them.'

'I'll put something on them quickly before I go,' I offered.

'Are you sure?'

'Yes, it'll only take me ten minutes. I'll lock up. Now on you go.' I shooed Joyce and Alma out. Both of them gave me a hug and then hurried out into the cold night wrapping their coats around them. I waved them off and then went upstairs to the storeroom and picked three dresses from the rails. I flicked the light off and then jumped when I heard a knock on the door downstairs. Joyce and Alma had sets of keys so I knew it wasn't them. Gilles perhaps?

With only the street lights illuminating the storeroom I peered out the window to see who it was. If it was Gilles, I told myself, I'd pretend I wasn't in. He'd no doubt be frisky and full of champagne.

But it wasn't Gilles.

The darkly dressed figure of Innes looked up at the window.

I stepped back, almost tumbling into one of the rails of glittering evening gowns. The sparkle from the sequin fabrics was enough to alert anyone that I was in.

I pressed myself against the edge of the window frame and had another peek. He was still there. He knew I was in.

I saw my reflection in the full–length mirror. I'd worn my hair down at the beginning of the night, with only two diamante clasps pinning up each side. In the whirlwind of helping customers in the shop, I'd tied it back in a ponytail. I pulled the hair band out and let my hair fall around my shoulders. Not that I was planning on enticing him. No, it was just that...well, I wanted to feel confident when I went downstairs to see what he wanted.

I clutched the three dresses on the hangers and held them in front of me like a shield as I unlocked the glass door.

He wore a dark coat with the collar turned up. It looked expensive and so did he. Everything about him had a type of class and strong, manly elegance.

'Can I talk to you, Bee?' His voice was deep and caused all sorts of flutterings inside me that I hoped I hid well.

'Yes.' I stepped aside and locked the door again as he walked into the shop. If ever a man didn't belong here...

His eyes flicked around, taking in everything. I could almost hear his mind process the data and come to some sort of conclusion. I sensed he didn't do this deliberately, but from habit, from training. A man who could sum up where he was and know how to handle anything that was thrown at him.

But could he identify a vintage cocktail dress from a little box pleat number? His eyes were on the dresses I was clutching.

I relaxed my grip but he'd already sussed that I was nervous or a little bit excited.

'I was about to put these on the mannequins,' I said. I smiled casually and stepped into the window. 'We've sold a lot of dresses and other clothes this evening. I'm sorting the window display ready for the morning.'

'I didn't mean to interrupt.'

'What did you want to talk to me about?'

I pulled one of the dresses over a mannequin and adjusted it. My heart pounded and I hoped he couldn't hear the nervous pitch in my voice.

'I wanted to explain where I'd been these past weeks.'

I glanced round at him. 'You don't owe me any explanation.'

The firm lips pressed together and then he said, 'I was hoping you'd have dinner with me tomorrow night.'

I knocked the mannequin against the window.

He rushed over and helped me steady it.

Would he steady me?

Now he was so near I didn't need to enlarge any picture of him to see his gorgeous green eyes in close–up. They were a breath away from me — and so were his sensual lips.

For the craziest moment I thought he was going to kiss me, but then he stepped back.

'So what do you think?' he said.

That I needed fresh air, that I wished the blush I could feel burning across my cheeks would calm down along with my heartbeat. And maybe, deep down, I wished he had kissed me.

I breathed and blamed the champagne Gilles had given me. But would one glass of pink champagne cause me to feel like this? I doubted it. Seeing Innes standing there in the shop created more excitement than was in that glass of bubbly.

'Will you have dinner with me, Bee?'

I nodded, fascinated by this man. Have dinner with him? Oh yes. And then I remembered. 'Gilles.'

The sweep of his brows arched as he looked at me.

Damn! Damn!

'I eh...I forgot that I already have a dinner invitation for tomorrow evening.' Rotten timing as always.

'Another time perhaps when I come back to Glasgow.'

'You're leaving?' A stab of disappointment went through me.

'That's why I wanted to see you before I left again. I've been in London and I have to go back again.'

'Why have you waited all this time to ask me to have dinner with you?'

'Because there were things that I had to do and I wasn't sure whether to become involved with someone again.'

I looked at him. 'Are you really what I think you are?'

He didn't reply.

'Do men like you have relationships?'

'Everyone's entitled to a private life.'

'Are you?'

'I will be.'

'When?'

'When I come back from London.'

'Are you coming back?'

'Yes.'

I knew he could be encouraging my imagination to think all sorts of things — that he was a secret agent and did lots of daring and adventurous things. 'How do I know you I can trust you? If your work is so secret, why didn't you tell me that you were a businessman or something like that?'

'Because it would've been a lie. And although I don't know you, I've liked you since I first saw you in the shop.' He frowned. 'Sometimes life is just too complicated to explain.'

I felt the tension build between us, pushing us apart. 'Tell me something about you.' Surely he could tell me something, anything that would help me to understand him better.

His features hardened as if I'd caused enormous conflict within him. 'Ask me one question and I'll answer it.'

I chose my question carefully. 'Why did you wear those heavy clothes in such hot weather and then wear less when it was cold?'

He hesitated. 'I'd been injured and was sent up here to recoup. I wore the clothes to cover up the injuries until they healed.'

'Is that why you were walking at first and then started running weeks later?'

He nodded.

'You were building up your strength, getting your fitness back after being injured?'

He nodded again.

36

Now it made sense. I wanted to ask what the injuries were but that seemed too personal and inappropriate.

'It was mainly cuts and bruises.'

'I'm sorry. I didn't know that you'd been hurt.'

He looked at me with eyes that melted my heart. 'It hurts more to think that I'm too late and that you're already involved with someone else.'

'I'm not. Gilles only asked me this evening at his party in the coffee shop if I'd have dinner with him. I said yes because...well...I thought you'd never ask me, and Joyce and Alma said that I should give Gilles a chance. I didn't tell the girls about you. Nothing secret, if you know what I mean.'

'He's the man who wouldn't give you back your camera?'

'Yes, he was fooling around with it...' Trying to take a photograph of you.

'Maybe you should give Gilles a chance.'

'You think I should have dinner with him?'

'No. I'm just being polite.'

I laughed.

'I'd like you to cancel dinner with him and have dinner with me.'

I would've done this but he added, 'But I don't think you should do that. Have dinner with Gilles and I'll see you when I get back from London.'

He smiled resignedly and headed towards the door.

I unlocked it. The cold night air blew into the shop.

He stood for a moment in the doorway.

Was he going to kiss me? He looked like he wanted to. Instead he smiled at me. 'Take care of yourself, Bee.'

'You too,' I said softly.

He walked away.

I watched him until he was just a shadow in the night. Then the figure turned at the far end of the street and waved to me. One last acknowledgment. I waved back to him.

Then he was gone.

I closed the door and shivered. Had I made the right decision? Had I?

I finished dressing the mannequins, flicked the lights off and drove home, wondering if I'd ever see Innes again or if that really was our last goodbye.

Chapter Five

Sewing & Knitting

Rain swept along the city streets. I sat at my sewing table upstairs in the workroom feeling safe and cosy in my little world of sewing and knitting.

I smoothed the floral print fabric out on the large table in the workroom and then cut the pattern pieces to make a dress.

Joyce and Alma were downstairs in the shop serving customers and sewing in spare minutes. All three of our sewing machines had been whirring busily all morning. There were new dresses, skirts and tops to make and items to upscale. And that was just the sewing.

Knitted stoles, wraps and cloche hats were needed for our winter accessories. We could all knit as well as sew, though Joyce was a seasoned expert and could knit beautiful lacework edging that gave the boleros she knitted a lovely vintage finish. Customers would often buy a hand knitted wrap or bolero to go with their evening dress purchase especially now that it was winter.

I'd told Joyce and Alma sketchy details about Innes during our morning tea break, and even then Joyce kept sewing at her machine while Alma unpicked a frayed ribbon trim from a dress neckline and I stitched a sequin appliqué on to one of our new designs.

By the afternoon we needed something delicious to keep us going as we'd hardly stopped all day. I threw on the raincoat I'd made, which was becoming a favourite of mine because it fitted so well. I'd allowed room in the upper part of the pattern so that I could wear a jumper or two without feeling bulky, and the length shielded my legs from the rain without being too long. I'd added a cosy lining for warmth and an old–fashioned fastener to keep the neckline closed against the wind and rain. Joyce had sourced a trench coat weight fabric in vintage pink and I'd used it to make my coat. When I tied the belt to cinch in the waist it was the loveliest and most flattering coat I'd ever worn.

I ran to Gilles shop to buy a cake. He smiled when he saw me.

I went up to the patisserie counter. 'We need cake.'

'Hectic day?'

I held out strands of my hair that had broken free from my up–do. 'Advance warning. I may not have time to arrive for dinner with anything less than a wild woman hairdo.'

'That's fine with me. Shall we say seven?'

'I'll be at the shop. We've got a lot of work to do and we're all working late.' I wouldn't need to go home to change. I planned to wear a dress I'd made from one of my vintage fabric designs.

Gilles helped me select the cakes. 'Can I suggest the frosted fairy cakes. The vanilla and raspberry ones are sweet and delicious.'

'I'll have those and three plain scones with jam and whipped cream. We're indulging.'

He gave me a sexy grin. 'I hope you'll indulge with me this evening.'

'Just dinner,' I reminded him. 'You promised.'

He held up his hands. 'I never renege on a promise.'

I smiled and scurried back to the shop, sheltering the cakes and scones from the rain.

Joyce was chatting to someone on the phone. I held up the cakes to show her what I'd bought. She gave me the thumbs up but seemed engrossed in the call.

'Was Gilles flirting with you?' Alma asked me.

'A little bit. He's picking me up here at seven.'

'What are you going to wear?' said Alma, following me through to the kitchen.

I put the cakes and scones on plates and poured the tea that was ready in the pot. A tea cosy that Joyce had knitted kept it warm. 'The dress I made from the painting print fabric. It's been hanging on the rail upstairs. I thought I'd give it a whirl.'

'I love that dress. You'll look great.'

Alma carried the tea tray through to the front shop. I put the plates of cakes and scones down on the little table behind the counter and we sat down to enjoy our tea break.

'Yes, Bee's here in the shop,' Joyce said to the caller. 'She's the one who designs the fabrics. Do you want to talk to her?' She listened to their reply and then handed the phone to me. 'It's the manager of the department store you used to work for. He's interested in selling our new fabrics in their haberdashery.'

What? I mouthed to her.

She held out the phone and nodded enthusiastically.

'Hello?' I said. 'Yes, Mr Greyson, I remember you.' We'd hardly ever spoken but he'd always been pleasant.

'One of our staff came in recently wearing a dress she'd made from fabric she'd bought from Joyce's shop. Everyone loved the dress pattern and the fabric. Joyce tells me you design them.'

'That's right.'

'We're always looking for something fresh and new for our store and we'd like to sell a collection of your fabrics in our haberdashery. I've spoken to Joyce about a fair price which she's happy with, but you'd also have to agree to this. We don't think that our store would take any trade away from your vintage shop. We think that it would have the opposite effect. We'd both benefit from increased sales.'

He went on to explain the details of the agreement. I felt so excited because he also wanted me to design a new range of ladies fashion for the department store.

'We ask various designers to come up with a capsule collection each season,' he said. 'At our marketing meeting we decided to give you the option to design several pieces for us — dresses for evening and daywear and skirts and tops.'

'Design a fashion collection for the department store?'

'Yes, Bee. We have one stipulation — and it's rather a difficult one, but we've had a few meetings and decided to put this to you.'

I held my breath.

'We'd like you to come up with something new. Use your new fabrics. Design others if necessary, but also create new styles for the clothes themselves.'

'Do you have a theme or anything like that in mind? I mean, that's quite a wide ranging request, Mr Greyson.'

'That, Bee, would be up to you. We won't put anything into production that we don't like, so everything would have to be approved at every stage of the design process, and we want it sooner rather than later. Joyce says we can have the fabrics right away, but we want those fashion designs pushed through as soon as possible to be included in our winter fashions. We have our own efficient production methods for our own range of clothing so what we'd do is give them a copy of your designs and they'd produce a limited collection exclusively for our store that we'd sell in our ladies clothing department. A few items would be available at Christmas time and others would be released for early spring next year. If the collection was popular, we'd extend our agreement to include further designs by you. Would you be agreeable to this?'

Would I? Is a squirrel's tail bushy? 'Yes. I certainly would.' If I could come up with the new designs. I handed the phone back to Joyce. She finished the call, agreeing that we'd meet with him in a couple of days to discuss the details. In the meantime, I was to push ahead with the designs.

We explained everything to Alma.

'Wow,' she said. 'That's so exciting.'

I was in need of a sit down, tea and cake. 'New designs,' I murmured, wondering what I could come up with.

'You can do it, Bee,' said Joyce.

Alma ate a fairy cake and nodded.

I drank my tea and took a moment for it all to sink in. I was sure I'd panic later, but right now the excitement was surging through me.

Joyce explained other things she'd discussed with the manager. 'I asked him why he came to us, a vintage shop, looking for new designs.'

'What did he say?' I asked her.

'He said that who better to know all the types of fashion styles that have already been used in the past than a shop like us. It's true. We've seen every decade spanning almost a hundred years. We know the fashions from the past. And so it makes sense to ask us, to ask you, Bee, with our help, to come up with a new collection.'

'I don't know that I can do that,' I said. 'I'll try of course. I'm definitely up for it.'

'What about that sketch book of yours?' said Alma. 'You're always scribbling ideas and designs in that. I've seen things I'd love to wear if only you'd make the patterns for them.'

'Let's have a look,' said Joyce.

I ran upstairs to the workroom. I kept my sketch book beside my sewing machine. I grabbed it and hurried downstairs.

Joyce flicked through the pages. 'Oh, Bee, these designs are wonderful.' She smiled at me. 'The manager said he'd sell our fabric regardless of whether you can create the new designs for the clothes or not.'

'So we've definitely got a deal for the fabric?' I said.

'Yes.'

'That sort of eases the pressure,' I said. 'At least we'd have the fabric collection. I'll certainly try to design the fashion collection. It's a small range of items.'

'We'll help you. Won't we Alma?'

Alma nodded and smiled at me. 'This is going to be so amazing.'

I brushed my hair, pinned it up in a barrette, freshened my makeup and put my dress on.

I looked out the window of the workroom at the rainy night. Boots would've been preferable to the T–bar shoes I was wearing. I shrugged on a cosy cardigan that had a pretty floral trim.

'Gilles is here,' Joyce called up to me. Alma had gone home and Joyce said she would finish up after I left.

I grabbed my raincoat and hurried downstairs.

Gilles was standing in the doorway dressed in a suit. His car was parked outside the shop with the engine running. 'You look lovely, Bee.'

I smiled and he helped me on with my coat.

Joyce waved us off. 'Enjoy yourselves, and don't do anything that I would do.'

I laughed and waved back at her.

Gilles turned the heater up and we drove across the city to the restaurant. I relaxed and gazed out at the streets.

'You're very quiet.'

I blinked out of my thoughts. 'Sorry, it's been a crazy day.' I told him about the department store deal.

'That's great.' He sounded really pleased for me which made me feel guilty that I was just going through the motions of going out with him when I'd have preferred to go home and work on the designs.

We arrived at the restaurant and were seated at a quiet table. The restaurant was new and I'd never been to it before, but Gilles had been invited to the opening and recommended it. We ordered from the menu. I hadn't realised I was so hungry until our dinner was served. I was just in the mood for fresh vegetables and chicken in the lightest of sauces.

'The flavours are marvellous,' I said.

Gilles was pleased. 'Now tell me more about this deal with the department store.'

During dinner I chatted about everything that I was supposed to do, about the fabrics, the designs and I continued to talk while Gilles listened and asked me things that men tended not to be interested in. Or maybe I just knew the wrong men. I'd never known a man to be fascinated to hear about my floral artwork or the finish on a hem. I prattled on until we'd almost finished the meal before finally shutting up.

'I'm sorry, Gilles. I haven't shut up all evening. You must be exhausted listening to me going on about the fabrics and fashions.'

He leaned closer and looked straight at me across the table. 'I'm interested to hear the things that interest you.' There was no hint of smarmy charm about him. I noticed that his eyes weren't the dark brown that I'd thought and were more hazel–brown and sparkled with warmth and humour.

'Tell me what interests you, Gilles.' I sat back ready to listen.

'Let me see...baking, cakes, coffee. Baking bread, rolls, scones.' He paused. 'Nope, that's all. My interests are narrow but I love what I do.'

'Any interests apart from your work?'

'My work is everything. You love dressmaking and design. I love cakes and coffee. My father is French and he has many interests — wine making, architecture, music. My mother is Scottish and she too has lots of interests — travelling, cooking. They live in France and would like me to settle there, marry and raise a family.'

'Will you do that?'

'No. I love living in Glasgow, and when I marry, I'll continue to work here.'

'Do you plan on expanding your business? Perhaps own more than one coffee shop?'

He shook his head. 'I'm happy to make a success of my shop. I make a lot of money, and yes, I could make more if I had other shops, but I don't want to spend all my time running around dealing with the business and having no time to relax. And I don't think women want a man who is never home. Some men seem fascinating and sexy if they have an exciting and adventurous career, but the reality is very different. I believe that women love having a man who comes home at night for his dinner and is there for them.'

'That's quite a sales pitch. I'm surprised you haven't been snapped up.'

He laughed. 'I've been waiting for the right woman.' He gazed across at me. 'What have you been waiting for?'

'I don't know. Happiness I suppose.'

'Joyce tells me that your ex boyfriend was a rat. Are you over him?'

'I am.'

He lowered his gaze and then looked across at me. 'What about your mystery man? Are you still interested in him?'

I sighed.

He leaned back in his chair. 'You know, there are few things sexier than a man who is strong and intriguing. A man who has a sense of danger and adventure about him. But ask yourself this — would this be the type of man who would be happy to be home and snuggled up cosy with you on a rainy evening like this? Or would he be away a lot of the time, working, travelling on business, never there with you?'

'You're right, Gilles.'

'And yet you still want him?'

I didn't know what to say to him, and my hesitation confirmed that I was interested in Innes and not him.

'I'm sorry, Gilles. I wish things were different.'

'Me too, and perhaps one day they will be.'

I was quiet for a moment and then I said, 'Alma really liked you. Did you know that?'

'No, I didn't.'

'She's dating someone now. I think she's happy with him.'

'So she doesn't care for me any more?'

I shrugged. 'She got fed up waiting.'

A waiter approached and served us our coffee.

'Let's not mope,' said Gilles when the waiter left.

'Agreed. Tell me about your new winter menu.'

'Well, I've added cognac to my chocolate cake...'

After dinner Gilles drove me back to the shop where I'd parked my car.

'Thanks for dinner, Gilles. I had a great time.' It was true. I'd enjoyed his company.

'Let's do it again sometime.'

I nodded.

44

As I went to get out of the car he said, 'One kiss.'

I looked at him, at his sexy smile and eyes that sparkled with warmth.

Without giving me time to think about it, he leaned over and kissed me. 'Goodnight, Bee.'

'Goodnight.'

I stepped out into the cold night with his kiss burning on my lips.

He waited until I was safely in my car before he drove off.

I let out a huge sigh and turned on the ignition. That's when I noticed a car parked further along the street facing me. The driver got out of the car and started to walk towards me.

'Innes,' I murmured. What was he doing here?

'I hoped you'd come back to the shop to pick up your car,' he said to me through the window.

'I thought you'd be heading to London by now.'

'I'm catching an early morning flight, but I wanted to see you again before I left. Can we talk?'

'Here?' I assumed he'd get into my car or we'd go inside the shop.

'No, I live nearby. I rent an apartment in the city centre. Can I offer you a nightcap before you go home?'

His handsome face and deep, sensual voice tempted me to follow him in my car to his apartment. Joyce was right. He lived a few streets away from the shop.

The rain had stopped but the air was freezing cold. My car barely had time to heat up before we pulled up to his apartment. He led the way inside.

He lived on the top floor in an exclusive apartment that overlooked the city.

I stood gazing out of the large glass doors that opened on to a rooftop balcony. The lights of the city shone in their thousands and the streets below glistened, still wet with rain.

Innes flicked the lights on, lamps that gave a glow to the neutral decor. I assumed he'd rented it furnished and decorated. It had that type of pristine look to it, like something you'd see in a glossy magazine.

The kitchen area was set alongside the lounge and I watched Innes take his jacket off and put it over the back of a chair. I took my coat off but wondered where to put it. The cream coloured sofa and chairs didn't seem ideal and there wasn't a lot else. I could've danced on the area of wooden flooring that started where the pale beige rug ended and the space leading up to the window view began. I liked the airy decor, softened by the subtle lighting. The view was worth seeing. I'd have loved to sew while gazing out over the city.

'Let me take that for you.' Innes swept my coat away. 'Would you like a drink or would you prefer coffee or tea?'

'Tea please.'

I stood beside the window and watched Innes prepare the tea. In the background, the city wrapped itself around me, a panoramic view of lights and energy.

'I know that you said I don't owe you any explanation,' he said, bringing the tea through to the lounge area, 'but there is something I want to tell you, to ask you, and I have to do it tonight before I leave for London. If your answer is no, then I promise you I will never bother you again.'

Chapter Six

Christmas Fabrics

'What do you want to ask me?'

Innes sat down on the sofa opposite me. 'Come with me to London.'

I hesitated. 'I...I can't go with you.'

He nodded as if he'd expected my reply.

I put my cup of tea down on the table and gazed at him. 'I'd like to, but I've been offered the chance to design my own fashions and fabrics for the department store I used to work for.' I explained the details.

He was nodding in agreement before I'd even finished. 'I understand. I'm sure you'll do well. I wish you every success.'

'When will you be coming back to Glasgow? You are coming back, aren't you?'

'The end of November.'

'I'll see you then?'

'Yes.' He sighed and stared into the depths of his cup. 'I was in London recently so that the department could check I was fit and well. I have one more fitness check before I resume my new duties.'

'For the department?' Okay, so I was fishing for more details. I didn't even know what the department was but it sounded official.

'I work for the Government. It wasn't my intention. I was approached when I was about to finish university. I chatted to them and they offered me the chance to work in their department in London. Working in intelligence. It sounded interesting and yes, exciting. I was younger then and I enjoyed the work at first. I liked working in the London office. Despite what you may think of me, I'm happier doing research and being office based rather than doing field work. However, due to my level of fitness and physical capability they asked me to transfer to field work, working abroad quite a bit.'

I sensed that if I interrupted him, he'd stall. I could already hear the hesitation as he chose his words carefully, revealing only what he thought I needed to know, so I let him continue.

'During my last assignment abroad, things went awry and I was injured before being brought back to London. I wasn't badly hurt, but I'd already asked to be transferred back to...I suppose you would call it a desk job. They agreed. I'm originally from Edinburgh though I've spent a considerable amount of time working in London and abroad, and they decided to send me up to Glasgow to regain my fitness and to see if I'd like working here.'

'They've got a department in Glasgow?'

'Yes. It's just Government work, but I'm keen to settle here. As I say, it was never my intention to work and travel all over the world.' He gazed at me. 'And it was never my intention to feel the way I do about you.'

I smiled at him. 'So what are we going to do?'

He got up and came over and sat beside me. 'I have to go to London, but I'm asking you to wait for me. Don't fall in love with anyone else, especially Gilles.'

'I don't love Gilles.'

'A lot of women do. Apparently he's quite the charmer — and bakes great cakes.'

'Someone's been doing their research,' I said.

'Damned bad habit of mine.'

'What other bad habits do you have?'

He leaned close and wrapped his arms around me. 'You. I can't stop thinking about you. You're a beautiful distraction. I find that when I should be concentrating on my work, I'm thinking about you — picturing you standing in the window of the shop watching me.' He laughed. 'And that day you ran after me in the rain — I'll remembered that forever.'

He pulled me even closer and whispered to me before he kissed me. 'Wait for me, Bee. Give me a chance. Give us a chance.'

I melted into him, returning the passion of his kisses with equal desire. 'Promise me you'll come back.'

'I promise.'

We snuggled up together on the sofa, chatting and getting to know each other a bit better, until the early hours of the morning. I fell asleep in his arms and woke up around 3:00 a.m. with the sound of the rain battering off the windows of the lounge.

'I have to go,' I said to him.

'I'll walk you down to your car.'

We said our goodbyes sheltering in the doorway as the rain poured down, blurring the street on that cold, wet night.

He promised to keep in touch with me. He would phone me, but I couldn't phone him. He couldn't give me a contact number until his transfer back to Glasgow was complete.

I hoped he would keep his promise to call me from London. I hoped for so many things including a chance for happiness with this elusive man who planned to start a new life soon. A new life that included me.

'Gilles must have made quite an impression on you,' Joyce remarked to me.

I was upstairs in the workroom sketching designs — and daydreaming about Innes and all that had happened the previous night.

'Gilles was good company but...he's not the man for me.'

'Are you sure?'

'Yes.'

She gave me a wry smile. 'Does this have something to do with Innes?'

'It has everything to do with Innes.'

She put a cup of tea down for me and a piece of shortbread. 'Well, here's a cuppa to keep you fired up to get those designs finished.' She smiled warmly and went to go back downstairs. We'd agreed that I would work like crazy to get the designs and fabrics ready for the department store while Joyce and Alma kept the shop going.

'Joyce?' I called to her.

She turned and looked at me.

'Would you ever get involved with a man whose past you didn't know all about and never really would?'

'Oh yes. Sometimes the past needs to belong where it is, in the past, and there's nothing to gain from raking over the old coals.'

'Thanks, Joyce.' She always made me feel better.

'It works both ways of course,' she added. 'Often it's the woman who has more secrets than her man. But that's when the rules of the game are in our favour. Women are allowed secrets. Men just think they are.'

49

We both laughed, and any pressure I'd felt about Innes and his past faded. I drank my tea, ate my shortbread and worked on my designs.

'The Christmas fabrics have arrived and they are brilliant,' said Alma. She spread them out on the haberdashery counter. Festive red, gold and green were the main colours, but Joyce had also ordered my Christmas fabric designs which included snowflakes on an ice blue background, a robin print and little Christmas trees in four different colours. 'I love your Christmas tree fabric, Bee. I'm having a dress made from that for the party season.'

'The prints have come out so well.' I ran my hands along the soft jersey fabric and cotton silk. The colours were brilliant and I pictured adding velvet ribbon trims to the dresses and tops I planned to make.

Alma cut a metre of the Christmas tree fabric to put out on display. 'Joyce told me that Gilles is still on the market.'

'Do you fancy asking Santa to gift Gilles to you for Christmas?' I said.

'Noooo. I'm happy with Colin.' Her eyes sparkled with enthusiasm. 'He's invited me to spend Christmas with him and his parents.'

'Getting serious, eh?'

'It certainly is. We get on really well. We want the same things in life. He wants to settle down and start a family.' She rolled up the Christmas fabrics and I helped her stack them on the shelves. 'I like working here but I have no notion to own my own business or to do the things that you do. I've always wanted to get married and have children and feel settled.'

Two customers who were browsing through the clothes rails spotted the new fabrics.

'I like those Christmas fabrics,' one of them said.

The other woman nodded. 'That Christmas tree material would make a lovely table runner. I'll have a couple of metres of that please, Alma.'

While Alma measured out the fabric and sold them thread and trims, I noticed that Joyce had dived behind the front shop counter. Then I saw the tailor she'd dated a couple of times looking in the window.

'Tell him I'm out,' Joyce whispered to me.

'I'm sorry. Joyce isn't in,' I called out to him.

He smiled tightly and walked away.

'He's gone. You can come out now.'

Joyce stood up. 'Thanks, Bee.' She sighed. 'He's been trying to persuade me to go out with him again but I'm not taking things any further.'

'I thought you liked him.'

'I did but he's getting too personal, wanting to know all about my past.' She adjusted her glasses. 'I'm happy with my shop and being able to do what I want without having to fit a man into my schedule. Sometimes I just want to go home and put my feet up, but he's on the phone asking to come round and take me out for a drink or a meal. And it complicates things. I wish he'd go away.'

'You need to stop hiding behind the counter,' one of the customers told Joyce.

'Yes,' Alma agreed. 'Once you've got to the hiding stage with a man it's time to tell him to get lost.'

'I think he knows you're not interested,' I said. 'He knew that you were in.'

'Do you have any pom poms?' a customer asked.

Joyce opened a drawer in the haberdashery counter. 'What colour, size and fluffiness were you looking for?'

I went back upstairs to push on with the designs. My sketch book was filled with pattern ideas, outlines for clothes, colours and textures. This saved me a lot of time and helped me put the designs together. I worked hard from early morning and continued working on them at night either at the shop or at home. I showed Joyce and Alma each pattern as I created the collection, and after a few meetings with Mr Greyson and others from his department store, we agreed on the final designs — six dresses, four skirts and six tops — with a theme of champagne chic lemonade money. Comfortable, classy and cost–effective designs.

The patterns and fabrics were sent away to the store's production team and samples were made quickly. These were then approved or altered until everything was ready to go into production. If this had been a normal process it would've taken months, but because the store already had a working team who were used to making small, select fashion collections of around twenty items in different colours and fabrics, they were able to do this efficiently in a few weeks.

I was sewing a gorgeous satin dress in the workshop one morning when Joyce called up to me. 'There's a call for you from London.'

'London?' I ran downstairs and grabbed the phone. I hadn't heard from Innes and was longing to hear his voice. 'Hello?'

But it wasn't Innes. It was Mr Greyson's marketing department in the store's London office. They wanted me to go down to have photographs taken to publicise the new fabrics and fashions.

Joyce and Alma helped me pack everything I needed and a few extras too. Joyce insisted I take a glamorous vintage evening dress. The bodice dripped with diamante and the skirt had layers of sparkling grey chiffon.

I caught a flight from Glasgow airport and within hours I was sitting in the department store's London office having photographs taken and giving them details of how I created the designs. They wanted to know everything about the process from my artwork to my pattern making. According to the marketing manager this was going to be used to promote the new range. Initial interest had been great, so they'd decided to include me in the publicity material.

They had a makeup artist and hair stylist to make me look presentable for the photographs which were taken in a studio by a professional photographer. It was fascinating to see what went on behind–the–scenes at this type of thing. I wore a dress I'd made from one of the fabrics that was going to be on sale in the store and a pair of rounded toe, low heel, classic shoes that I'd covered with the same fabric as the dress. The original shoes were scuffed so I'd renewed them myself. The marketing team were so taken with them that they wanted them included in the photographs. I was pictured standing beside a table laden with my fabric designs and pattern pieces. I'd brought my sketch book with me and that was included in some of the shots. They also took close–ups of my design illustrations — from the initial outlines to the finished fashion artwork. They were particularly pleased with these as they said the fashion illustrations would add interest to the features and show how I'd created the designs. The features were going to be on the department store's website, included in press releases and in their newsletter that was sent out to their customers, and as part of the company's general advertising.

The photo session lasted for hours but the time zipped by. My hair and makeup were continually titivated, lighting altered, fabric selection changed, and there was plenty of tea, biscuits, chatter and gossip.

During this, I was interviewed about my work, and they phoned Joyce to ask for her input for the editorial.

We finally finished at around seven in the evening. The marketing manager wanted me to come back the following day, Friday, to make a short video.

'We'd like you to sketch dress illustrations, work on a dress pattern showing how you make the paper pattern, that type of thing, and then cut out the fabric. We'll also include you sewing one of the seams. We'll have a sewing machine set up for you in the morning.'

Apparently the videos were popular with their customers who enjoyed watching them on the company's website, so I was expected to do this. Although I'd never been filmed while I worked, I was used to people watching me sew or design. When I worked in the department store I was right in the centre of things and became accustomed to people peering over my shoulder. This had continued in Joyce's shop. I often used the sewing machine beside the front counter while customers watched me. They'd ask for sewing tips and I was happy to advise them.

'We'll see you again at 10:00 a.m. in the morning,' said the marketing manager.

'I'll be here,' I confirmed.

They'd booked me into a hotel in the centre of London.

I'd just flopped down on the bed in my room when my phone rang. This time it was Innes. My senses soared. I couldn't wait to tell him that I was in London.

'I've missed you, Bee,' he said.

My heart squeezed at the sound of his voice. 'I've missed you too. Are you still in London?'

'I've been abroad for a couple of weeks. That's why I didn't call you sooner. However, I'm in London now.'

'So am I.' I was so excited to tell him this.

'You're in London?'

'Yes.' I told him about the publicity for the store.

'That's wonderful. Can we have dinner tonight or are you working?'

'I've finished working. They've booked me into a hotel in London.' I told him where I was staying. 'I just got back to the hotel. I was planning on ordering room service.'

'Forget room service. Have dinner with me. I know the hotel. I can be there in half an hour.'

'Okay, see you soon.'

I put a little sequin evening dress on, brushed my hair and toned down the makeup from the photo shoot. From looking at the previews, the photographs would be very flattering, but I wasn't used to wearing quite so much foundation, and knowing how I'd react seeing Innes, I wouldn't need any blusher.

Within half an hour I heard Innes knock on my room door. Oh the butterflies that fluttered through me.

I smoothed my dress down, took a deep breath and opened the door.

When I saw him standing there dressed in one of the sharpest suits I'd ever seen, I needed every bit of that breath. Innes was gorgeous. My heart ached just looking at him, especially when he smiled at me.

'It's great to see you again, Bee.'

We held each other close and he kissed me with such passion that I forgot about everything except how I felt when I was in his arms.

He finally released me from his embrace and I picked up my coat and my bag.

'I've booked a table at a restaurant I hope you'll like.' He held his arm out, I linked mine through his, and off we went.

Chapter Seven

Diamonds & Deception

The restaurant was exclusive and had a traditional decor. I think he'd chosen it hoping I'd appreciate the vintage feel to it. It had old world style and charm — as did Innes.

'How long are you going to be in London?' he said as we selected from the menu.

'Four days. I arrived today and I have to film a short video they're making tomorrow for their marketing and publicity.' I told him all about it. 'I also have to meet with their marketing manager again. I thought I'd be here for two days, but they've extended the hotel booking from Thursday and Friday to include Saturday and Sunday. I fly back to Glasgow on Monday morning. It's like a mini holiday. I'm so glad that you phoned. It would've been awful to have missed seeing you.'

He nodded, and then his smile faltered.

'What's wrong, Innes?'

'I was planning to ask you to fly down to London. There's a function that I have to attend on Saturday — a dinner dance in one of the city's hotels.'

This sounded okay. Why did he looked concerned?

'I have to attend. It's something that's part of my job. There are a few things that I have to do before I can leave London and start working in Glasgow.'

'What's the problem then? I'm in London. It's a dinner dance. I have a dress that's suitable. Joyce insisted I bring it with me from the shop.' It was a genuine vintage evening dress that sparkled like something out of a fairytale and yet skimmed my figure in the most flattering way. But it was the movement of the fabric, the sparkle of chiffon over the skirt as if someone had sprinkled it with starlight that made me love it. It was a dress that moved so beautifully. A dress that was made for dancing at a party like this.

'The problem is — I need to borrow a fiancée for the evening. The people who are there have to believe that I'm engaged. And I was wondering...could you pretend to be my fiancée for one night?

It's not something dangerous that I'm getting you involved in. But you'd have to pretend that you were in love with me.'

No stretch there I thought.

I smiled and teased him. 'That's quite an acting job you're offering me. But I suppose I can pretend that I think you're handsome and wonderful.'

He laughed. 'So you'll do it?'

'Yes, Innes. I will.'

After dinner we drove through London, cocooned in our own little world, talking about all the things we wanted to do and the things that we had to do before we could do what we wanted.

His car was black, a shadow that I saw in the shop windows as we drove past. Inside felt luxurious and I relaxed into the expensive comfort of it, allowing the sights and senses to flicker over me. I hadn't been in London for years and I enjoyed seeing what it looked like these days.

We made plans that I wasn't sure we would keep, but I liked the feeling of planning a future with Innes.

'Would you like to go for a sail along the Thames on Sunday?' he said. 'We could have lunch on the boat.'

'I'd love that.'

'I'll make a booking for us.'

I smiled brightly. 'That's a date then.'

He reached over and gave my hand a squeeze. 'Every day would be a date if I had my way.'

We drove through the centre of London that was alive with activity. The theatres were aglow with lights and I recognised many of the famous landmarks as we drove across the bridges. Innes pointed out where we'd embark on our boat trip. The water on the Thames was smooth and dark like liquid liquorice and the city's colourful lights reflected on the surface. The artist in me saw potential to make a fabric design — flashes of warm, bold colour, amber, red, golden yellow, on a rich midnight background.

'I know you have to go back to the hotel because you're working tomorrow morning, Bee, but would you like to come for a nightcap with me?'

'To your house?' I tried and failed to contain my enthusiasm. Oh how I wanted to see where Innes lived to understand more about him.

'I have a place in London. It's actually not far from your hotel.'

And so he drove me to his place — a substantial apartment in a traditional building. Again, he lived on the top floor, but that's where any similarity to his apartment in Glasgow ceased. This place reminded me of something you'd see in a film where the adventurous professor lived surrounded by books and maps and a study with leather chairs on either side of the fireplace. Old–fashioned table lamps cast a warm light and rugs with subdued patterns covered the polished wood flooring. Everything was polished, clean, busy but tidy. A sturdy oak desk bore the weight of two laptops, a printer, various computer and tech stuff, along with two vast volumes of maps of the world — one including the past showing how the world used to be and the other present world maps. He let me flick through them.

I stood there looking around while Innes sparked a match and lit the fire. It burst into flames and began to crackle. I was thankful for the sound because the room was so quiet. No noise from the streets filtered up and through to Innes' domain above the city. I felt he'd hear my heart beating with excitement.

'I've never been in a room like this.' I'd thought this in my mind but inadvertently spoke my thoughts aloud.

'I'll make us tea,' he said, smiling.

I took my coat off and put it over the back of one of the leather chairs.

I wandered around, noting that the books were non–fiction, covering everything from world history to marine engineering. Was this why he'd suggested the boat trip? Was he interested in the sea? Then I saw books on mountaineering, on classical art. He had two paintings on the wall that fought for space against the large maps of the world that were framed and hung opposite the fireplace. Above the fireplace was a painting of a city harbour at night, old docks from the 1800s. I could see why he liked it. It made me feel calm just looking at it, at a piece of the past where life seemed less complicated.

Innes brought the tea through. I'd been so absorbed in my thoughts I hadn't even heard him make it. He'd taken his jacket off and loosened his tie, but even dressed like this Innes was far from casual. Casual as a male model would be to advertise top quality menswear. Pinch me, I was dreaming. I was really tucked up in bed in Glasgow and due to work in Joyce's shop in the morning.

Innes kissed me and put the tray of tea and cake down on the table in front of the fire.

Nope, no dream was this delicious. And I wasn't meaning the cake. Innes kissed me as a man would who really did love a woman and was at ease with her, with himself.

'I can't compete with Gilles' baking, and I won't pretend that I baked this cake, but my weekly grocery order was delivered today and so...' he pointed to the Victoria sponge cake he'd sliced and put on two plates for us.

Even his choice of cakes was traditional. If he had an old–fashioned bath, one that was deep and large enough for two to luxuriate in, and plenty of wardrobe space in the bedroom, I was moving in. The real fire and cosiness of the living room/study was a major tick–box for me. I wanted to see the kitchen but didn't dare. If it had an antique dresser and other things I loved I'd never leave.

I laughed as we sat on either side of the fireplace sipping tea and eating cake. 'This is so civilised.'

His eyes flicked around the room. 'Is this what you expected?'

I smiled and shook my head. It was nothing like I'd expected. I wished I had Joyce's ability to analyse things. What would she think of it all? I'd been asking her to teach me the skill to suss people out by the clothes they wore, their manner, the things they owned. She was a natural at this, but I'd picked up some tips and learned from her that first impressions counted whether they were created for show, like wearing a beautiful gown to a party, or whether they were part of a person's lifestyle such as a dressmaker buying fabric to sew. Everything told a story about who we were and what we did — and sometimes...sometimes gave a glimpse of what we aspired to be.

We drank our tea by the fireside and he asked me about my designs. We chatted for about an hour and then he drove me back to the hotel. I needed to get some sleep because I had a busy day ahead.

'I'll call you tomorrow night,' he said. 'I hope the video goes well.'

'Thanks, Innes.' I paused and then asked him, 'Why do you want me to accompany you to the party on Saturday and not a woman who works with you at the department? Not that I don't want to go with you. I do. I just wondered.'

'The people at the dinner dance would know she didn't love me. I'm not implying that you do, but I'd like to think that you have feelings for me, enough to convince them that we were planning to get married.'

I smiled up at him. 'I think I can do that.' I wore a sparkly little ring on my right hand. It was a piece of fashion jewellery, nothing expensive. I slipped it on to my engagement ring finger. 'This would pass as an engagement ring.'

He frowned. 'It could but...' He held my hand and slipped the ring off. 'Can I take this with me?'

'Yes.'

He put it in his jacket pocket.

We kissed goodnight in the foyer of the hotel and then I went up to my room. I got ready for bed, flicked the lights off and gazed out at the view of London. And I thought about Innes. On Saturday I'd pretend to be his fiancée. Would he have a diamond ring for me to wear? I assumed he'd taken my ring so that he'd have the correct size. There were so many things to think about but I needed to get some sleep. I pulled the bed covers around me. The room was cosy but the night outside was freezing cold. Frost glittered on the rooftops that I could see as I lay in bed. Shops already had their Christmas decorations up. I fell asleep thinking about what I'd wear for the video, about all the shops in London that I wanted to see before I flew back to Glasgow, and I thought about Innes. I was looking forward to being engaged to him for one special night.

I got up early, showered and dressed for the day ahead. I'd washed my hair and thankfully it had dried smooth and silky. The hair stylist would no doubt do something amazing with it.

I wore my favourite white linen blouse, a real vintage piece, that had whitework embroidery on the cap sleeves. I also wore a tailored waistcoat I'd made in a subtle plaid that suited my straight, knee–length dark skirt.

I had breakfast in my room and then headed to the department store to work on the video.

'Love the outfit,' the marketing manager said to me. 'That's the type of look we had in mind for the video.'

The hair stylist brushed my hair but kept it loose so it was just my makeup that needed applied. I started to feel quite nervous when I saw that they'd arranged a makeshift sewing area where I was to stitch one of the dresses from the collection and show them how I sketched and designed the patterns.

'Don't be nervous, Bee,' one of the marketing team advised me. 'Just do what you do. We'll film plenty of footage and cut out any bits that don't work.'

I took a deep breath. Okay. I could do this. I did this every day without any fuss. The only difference was that I was surrounded by several people, had bright lights to contend with, clicking cameras, a film cameraman, and had to make my work process look interesting. No pressure.

Somehow I managed to do what they asked and we finished just after lunchtime. Phew!

I had lunch with the marketing manager who wanted to discuss a few details before I was free to enjoy the rest of the weekend in London. We talked about the publicity they planned and hoped that I would agree to be available for further interviews if needed, especially if the press picked up on the collection. Mainly, we were relying on the feature for the website. This was where the video would be shown to encourage customers to purchase items from the collection and let them see how I'd designed them.

Finally, I was released into the wild, and hit the shops in London in a whirlwind of excitement. I'd promised Joyce that I would check out some of the vintage shops in central London, along with the large department stores fashions. I basically shopped until I dropped.

It was early evening when I got back to the hotel. I flopped down on the bed, kicked my shoes off and thought about having dinner. I hadn't had anything since lunch, and even then I'd been so busy chatting to the marketing manager that I'd barely eaten anything. My tummy rumbled. I'd stopped while shopping to grab a tea but hadn't bothered to have a proper tea break.

I was about to phone for room service when Innes called.

'How did the video go?'

'Great.'

He laughed. 'You sound pleasantly exhausted.'

'I've been shopping. Fashion shopping.' I explained what I'd been up to.

'Can I entice you to have dinner with me?'

'No enticing required.'

'I'll pick you up in a few minutes.'

Innes took me to a restaurant that served the most delicious traditional food. I had steak pie with roast potatoes, followed by bread and butter pudding and custard.

After dinner we went into the cocktail lounge that had an outstanding view of the city.

'I have to work later tonight,' he said.

'That's okay. I've had a brilliant but exhausting day. I should get a proper night's sleep.'

'I'll pick you up at the hotel tomorrow evening at around seven.' He brought a small velvet box from his pocket and put it down on the table in front of me. 'I hope you like it.'

I opened the box and there was a scintillating diamond engagement ring. The diamonds were real and set in gold. I blinked a few times and it was Innes who took charge of the ring and put it on my finger. It fitted of course, being based on my own ring. 'It's beautiful.'

'I wasn't sure whether you'd prefer a solitaire or something like this. This was my choice. I'm pleased that you like it.'

'Like it? I love it.' I held my hand out so that the diamonds sparkled under the lights. 'It's the most beautiful ring I've ever worn. I'll be sorry when I have to give it back. I'm not hinting that I want it,' I said quickly, hoping he didn't think that I wanted it as payment for accompanying him. The ring must've cost thousands.

Innes took my hand and clasped it in his. 'I want to thank you, Bee.'

'What for?'

'For trusting me. For trusting someone who can't tell you everything about their life, even though I want to, but never can.'

'I understand. And it's okay. Besides, everything will be a bit different once you're transferred to the department's office in Glasgow. In the meantime, I'll force myself to wear this dazzling diamond ring, pretend to be your fiancée and attend a glamorous party with you tomorrow night.' I sighed and smiled. 'It's a hard life.'

He kept a hold of my hand. 'It's a complicated one.'

'It is, but I'd rather have that than never have known you.'

This was the first time those fabulous eyes of his looked deep emerald rather than the light, sharp green that could see right through me. 'Whatever happens, I want you to know that you're the best thing that's ever happened to me.'

People were getting up to dance, slow dancing in a designated area of the cocktail lounge.

Innes stood up. 'Shall we?'

We danced to the slow, romantic music. He held me close and was a much better dancer than me. I danced fine, but Innes led me well.

'Will we be dancing tomorrow night?' I asked him.

'Yes, so wear your dancing shoes.'

'I will.'

I'd brought a pair of my favourite shoes with me to London. They'd been a bargain because they were a bit worn. I'd seen the potential in them, and after cleaning and spraying the heels with glitter, they were perfect and oh so comfortable. I suspected they'd been made for dancing and the heels were an ideal height.

'Is there anything else you can tell me about the dinner dance?'

'Guests are expected to arrive between seven and seven–thirty. Dinner is served at eight. When the meal finishes couples will take to the dance floor. The hotel has an entire suite for this type of function. Security is tight. Only those with invitations are allowed in. Not hotel guests unless they're on the list.'

'Is this an annual event? Whose party is it?'

His reply was indirect. 'There will be a lot of diplomats and those in positions of power, especially in business.'

'It sounds like a bit of a power game.'

'Many things are. Even in your world, Bee. It just depends on what arena you're competing in.'

'And tomorrow's party is the major league?'

He nodded. 'Stick close to me, especially when we arrive.'

I smiled up at him as we danced together. 'I think I can handle that.'

He bent his head down and kissed me lightly.

'You'll be introduced as my fiancée. We'll be introduced to quite a few people when we arrive, but there's one man in particular who needs to see that we're a couple in love.'

'Who is he?'

'He's part of the main reason for the deception. He's tall with dark hair and has cold blue eyes.' He gave me no further details.

'What will I say if he asks me who I am and what I do?'

'I'll try to field off the questions. That's why you need to stick close to me. As you have no experience of this type of task, we'll use your real name, Bedelia. If he asks, tell him you work in fashion and leave it at that. Don't embellish or give him details if you don't have to.'

'He'll know from my accent that I'm Scottish.'

'Pretend you're based in Aberdeen. Don't tell him or anyone else anything unless it's absolutely necessary or look like you're lying. Tell the truth rather than come across as a fake.' He pulled me closer as we danced. 'But it shouldn't even come to that. It's me they're interested in and my background has been painted to include a fiancée. If we look like we're in love, everything will take care of itself. We're there to give the right impression. I'm supposed to be a businessman who travels a lot and has a substantial amount of wealth at my disposal.'

I glanced at my hand on his shoulder as we danced. The diamond ring sparkled like white fire. It was the type of ring anyone would expect a man of his status would give his fiancée. If I wore it with the evening dress, the classic shoes that had been made for dancing, and showed my true feelings for Innes, we could do this. We could.

Chapter Eight

Lemonade Money

Innes dropped me off at my hotel promising to pick me up again on Saturday night.

It wasn't that late, and I sat on top of my bed checking the emails on my laptop. I fired one off to Joyce telling her all about the video and photo shoot, and then settled down to draw some pattern ideas in my sketch book. I wished that I had brought my knitting with me. Knitting always helped me to relax and unwind, but as my mind was filled with fresh ideas for designs, I made myself a cup of tea and sketched some patterns.

My laptop was open on the bedside table and a reply arrived from Joyce, followed by a phone call from her. She was working late in the shop.

'We've had a busy day, Bee. Customers have been buying our new Christmas fabrics and patterns. Alma and I are putting up the Christmas tree and decorations. I always put my green tinsel tree in the front window. I've had it since the sixties and it's a lovely tree. We've covered it in two sets of colourful fairy lights and we've got lights all round the window. The shop's looking very festive. Alma's sticking a fairy on top of the tree.'

'Can she hear me?'

'No.'

'I bought her two pairs of fifties style bows from one of the shops in London. You know how she loves to clip bows to her shoes.'

'She'll love them,' Joyce whispered.

'Love what?' I heard Alma call.

'Just sort the fairy Alma,' Joyce told her. 'Fluff her wee dress out. It's been flattened being in the box with all the other decorations.'

'Has Bee been buying us pressies in London?'

'Tell her it's a surprise.'

'Bee says it's a surprise.'

'Okay,' she said to Joyce. 'And thanks, Bee.'

We laughed.

I told Joyce all about the marketing meeting and everything that had happened regarding the designs. And about Innes.

'A dinner dance?' Joyce sounded impressed.

'Thanks for packing that evening gown for me. It's going to come in handy.'

'I thought you'd need something glamorous in case the marketing people invited you to a posh party.'

'Well, I'm wearing it tomorrow night.'

'You'll look beautiful. And no one will have a dress like it. It's the only one of its kind. Hardly ever worn, though it did have a couple of outings to dinner dances.'

'I love it when you know the background details of a dress.' And then it dawned on me. The stitching, the scattering of sequins. 'Joyce, was this your dress? Did you make it?'

'I did. A long time ago obviously, but classics never go out of fashion. The hem got ruined one night in the rain so I shortened it slightly. That's why it's an ideal length for you now.'

'I wondered why I hadn't seen it in the shop's stock.'

Joyce laughed. 'You're not the only one to have wardrobes at home packed with the past.'

'Thanks again, Joyce. I'll take great care of it.'

'Don't fuss about that. Dresses are made to be worn. Dance and enjoy your party, Bee.'

'I'll snap pictures at the party so you and Alma can see all the glamour,' I said.

Joyce sounded hesitant. 'Maybe think twice about taking photos. Some of the guests may not want their pictures taken, especially if it's a very upmarket party.'

'Yes, you're right.'

'Take some pictures in your hotel room. Let us see what you look like before you go to the ball.'

'I'll do that, Joyce.'

'Oh and before I forget,' she added, 'Gilles told me to tell you he's asking for you.'

'I've only been gone two days.'

'You know what he's like. And remember, Gilles does like you, Bee.'

'Okay, tell him I'm having a great time in London and that I'm asking for him too.'

65

'I'll tell him,' said Joyce. 'But I'll need to go. Alma's trying to hang up a set of fairy light lanterns above the counter. It's an accident waiting to happen. Enjoy your party.'

I laughed and then settled back down to finish my cup of tea and sketch until I felt tired enough to get some sleep. I planned to go shopping for clothes bargains early on Saturday morning, then relax in the afternoon at the hotel so that I wouldn't be knackered for my party night with Innes.

I kept to my plan, even though the shops in London tempted me to shop all afternoon. The day whizzed by and soon I was styling my hair and adding rollers to give it some soft curls before putting on my dress and waiting for Innes to arrive. I wore my hair down and emphasised my eyes with grey and silver eye shadow and black mascara.

Knowing that the dress had belonged to Joyce made me feel even more comfortable in it. She was such a first–class dressmaker and the fabric felt gorgeous. It was the most beautiful evening dress I'd ever worn.

I checked the time. Innes would be here soon. I picked up my clutch bag — a lovely beaded, shell–shaped bag and took a picture of myself in the mirror with my phone. I sent a copy of it to Joyce. It was a great example of champagne chic lemonade money. Obviously, the dress was borrowed, but I could've worn another bargain evening dress from the past. A dress than no one else at the party would have. That was part of the beauty of wearing vintage — no one else wore the same. You could wear your own unique style on a budget. The shoes were a snip and the bag cost me very little. For button prices I looked like I'd spent a fortune on my outfit when it had really only cost me lemonade money.

I put the engagement ring on. Hmm...I was probably wearing the down payment of a house on my finger.

Innes arrived minutes later. He looked immaculate in a dark dinner suit. My heart ached when I saw him standing in the doorway smiling at me.

'You look really stunning, Bee.'

My heart lifted. 'Joyce made this dress.' I swished the fabric of the chiffon shirt, causing it to sparkle like stardust.

'It's beautiful, and so are you.'

I draped my coat around my shoulders and we headed out of the hotel to the party.

Lots of guests were arriving and we joined them. Innes was nodded to by various men as we entered the function suite where the party was being held. The ceiling dripped with chandeliers and the dining tables were set with polished silverware and crystal glasses. Very classy.

A large Christmas tree took pride of place in the far corner of the suite opposite the dance floor. Guests were milling around the bar areas and were being offered glasses of champagne from the waiting staff.

I held on to Innes' arm as we walked into the hub of the party. The engagement ring sparkled on my hand and for a moment, just a moment, I wanted to believe that I was there with Innes simply to enjoy myself without the shadow of pretence making me feel nervous.

Innes squeezed my hand. 'Are you okay?'

'Yes. I just hope that no one susses that I'm not really your fiancée.' I kept a fixed smile on my face as I spoke.

He leaned down and kissed me, brief, gentle, lovingly.

I gazed deep into his eyes as he pulled away again. He did love me, I thought. He really did.

I was introduced to several couples as Innes' fiancée. No one showed any sign that they disbelieved us. I began to relax but only for a few minutes because I suddenly felt a shiver go through me. A feeling of...I wasn't sure...danger, wariness.

Moments later, I was aware of someone approaching us. A man. As tall as Innes but leaner, handsome with sharp, pale features and an aristocratic demeanour. He wore a dinner suit, and a beautiful woman who had draped herself around him. Her dress was gold and matched the excessive jewellery she wore that I sensed from her attitude someone had lavished on her.

The shiver I felt gripped me again, and as this man drew nearer, I realised that it was him. Whatever it was about him, he made me wary in a way I'd rarely experienced. I wanted to step back, to avoid meeting him, but it was obvious he knew Innes and wanted to be introduced.

I felt the muscles in Innes' arm tense beneath my fingers. I gave his arm an acknowledging squeeze. He glanced at me, and I understood. This man was the main reason we were here.

I took a deep breath and made sure that my ring was visible as I linked my arm through Innes' arm. I tried to look relaxed while feeling the complete opposite.

'Ah, Innes,' the man said. His accent sounded French with an international flavour within his tone. 'I'm glad you could come here this evening. I wasn't sure that you would make it.' The cold blue eyes turned their penetrating gaze towards me.

Innes smiled casually and introduced me. 'This is my fiancée, Bedelia.'

An elegant hand reached out to shake mine. His hand felt warm to the touch and yet I felt nothing but coldness from him. I smiled anyway. 'Pleased to meet you.'

'This is Philippe,' Innes added.

Neither of them made any attempt to introduce the woman. This didn't seem to bother her in the slightest. In the oddest way I wished that I could be like her this evening, blend into the background, be able to enjoy the party without anyone wanting to know who I was.

The moment passed.

'I believe we're being seated for dinner,' said Philippe, gesturing towards one of the tables.

My heart sank. Oh no, we were seated at the same table as him, along with two other couples. They looked amiable enough, but Philippe...he was my idea of the perfect appetite suppressant.

Philippe led the way over to the table.

I glanced at Innes. He gave me a knowing look, and then produced a smile that only I knew was fake.

My heart sank further. What had I got myself into?

Philippe wangled the seating to make sure I was directly opposite him. He steepled his fingers and rested his chin on the tips. 'I was intrigued to know what type of woman had captured Innes' heart.'

Silence at the table. Everyone waited on my response. Oh gawd.

'It wasn't easy.' I smiled and hoped he'd focus on something else. Where were the menus when you needed them?

Philippe didn't falter. 'Do tell. I enjoy hearing how couples get together.'

I was drowning in panic. Innes had yet to dive in to save me. I had to flounder on my own.

Silence again. My turn to twist in the wind. My mind flicked through the options. Lie. No. Innes was adamant that they, whoever they were, could spot a lie instantly. So I gave him a version of the truth. No one could make our story up.

'I was dressing mannequins with vintage fashion in a shop window when I first saw him,' I began. 'During the course of a number of weeks I watched and admired him. Then one day I decided to run after him through the city streets in the rain.'

For the first time I noticed surprise register in Philippe's cold eyes. He hadn't expected that reply.

'And what happened?' Philippe said, glancing at Innes and then back to full focus on me. 'Did you catch him?'

I smiled. 'I do believe I did.'

Philippe clapped his hands. 'Bravo. I love a happy ending.' Then he frowned. 'Though perhaps your story is still unfinished. A woman of your beauty and charm may be stolen away by another man before you tie the knot.'

I heard the splash as Innes dived in to the conversation. 'That would his mistake.' Intense green eyes clashed with the cold blue look that Philippe gave him across the table.

Well, that really set the mood for dinner.

Thankfully the waiting staff arrived with the menus. Everything was presented so courteously.

Philippe shook off the challenge and smiled. 'Isn't this delightful. I do love events at this time of year. So festive.'

'So do I. I love Christmas.' Perhaps I shouldn't have spoken but the words were out.

'Tell me more about being in that shop window, Bedelia,' said Philippe. 'What were you doing there apart from dressing mannequins? What line of work are you in?'

'I'm a vintage dressmaker and pattern designer.'

Philippe's eyes flashed with interest. Genuine interest. Nothing about me matched what he'd been anticipating. The concern for me was why he was so keen to know my background. I suspected it was to test the authenticity of Innes' background cover as a high–powered businessman and not a secret squirrel who worked for the Government.

'Vintage clothes?' Philippe eyed my dress. 'That explains the classic beauty of your evening dress. And perhaps the woman who is wearing it.'

He'd overstepped the mark as far as Innes was concerned, but that was surely what he wanted. I'd never met a man of his coldness and power, but I understood the game play. He was trying to bait Innes. And that irritated the hell out of me. It reminded me of my ex and how he enjoyed messing with people's feelings, especially mine, for his own amusement. It triggered the past that I'd forgotten about for months. Bastard.

Under the table I gave Innes' hand a reassuring squeeze. Don't bite, I tried to urge him. Don't take the bait.

Innes got my message and remained quiet.

Philippe brushed an invisible speck of lint from the arm of his jacket. 'This suit was designed for me by my tailor. It's based on a classic thirties dinner suit. You can't beat the classics.' The pomposity puffed around him.

I frowned. 'Thirties? Really? Those lapels are late forties surely. And the top stitching on the cuffs places it firmly in the nineties rather than true vintage.' I shook my head in disapproval. 'And that buttonhole technique wasn't available until the seventies.' To be fair, only those who knew about clothes or worked in the industry would've sussed this. The suit looked impeccable.

Philippe's reaction wasn't pretty. He looked at his suit as if it had a stink.

Innes gave me a glance of disbelief. Had I just insulted this man?

The other couples concentrated on the menus and polite chatter filled the void where the silence had been. They pretended there wasn't a sense that I'd retaliated against Philippe and we were on the verge of verbal fisticuffs.

I softened my assessment of his suit, but not by much. 'I assumed it was a well–made mix of eras rather than a deliberate mistake and clash of decades in menswear.'

I couldn't help it. I blamed the two glasses of champagne I'd had since we arrived. And I blamed Innes for bringing me into this tinder box of trouble. He must've known that Philippe would single me out for an inquisition.

Anyway...Philippe wasn't happy and everyone at the table knew it.

A member of the hotel staff approached Innes. 'There's a call for you in reception, Sir.'

'Thank you, I'll be right there.' Innes stood up. 'Excuse me.' He glanced at me. 'I'll be back in a few minutes. Order for me. You know what I like.'

Realising that Innes would be out of the game for a little while, Philippe's ire was replaced with potential. I could see it on his face. I could read Philippe's type far easier than I could read Innes. This made me think that Philippe wasn't a secret agent but a man in business, in power, with wealth, who was probably up to financial mischief and that's why Innes was on his case. Or maybe he was just an awkward type and I was totally wrong. I preferred the former option and went with that one. No lemonade money in Philippe's world. It was champagne all the way.

Chapter Nine

The Romance Of Classic Clothes

Innes had barely left the table when Philippe stood up and held out his hand to me. 'Would you care to dance?'

I looked up at him. Was he kidding? We hadn't even had dinner yet. He smiled, cold, calculating. No, he wasn't kidding. I decided to take him up on his offer rather than be questioned any further while Innes was gone. Philippe couldn't waltz and question me at the same time. Could he?

We were the only couple on the dance floor. I think he hoped that this would make me feel embarrassed, but it was preferable to sitting at the table with the other strangers pretending that everything was fine.

'People are watching us,' he said. 'Watching you. That dress you're wearing is exquisite. Vintage no doubt.'

'Genuine vintage.'

'Ouch,' he said, feigning injury from my jibe and not my dancing.

The music rose to a stronger beat and he waltzed me around the floor. He was a better dancer than me. I kept up okay and my dress hid any awkward footwork. I caught a glimpse of us dancing in the full length windows at the far end of the dance floor. My dress sparkled so much I could hardly see where the fabric started and finished. It was all a fairytale haze of chiffon and starlight. I loved the romance of classic clothes.

The music calmed again and we slowed down. Philippe held me close as we waltzed gently. He whispered in my ear. 'You excite me. I've never met a woman like you.'

Judging by the soigné figure draped in gold sipping champagne cocktails at the dinner table and not giving a hoot about me dancing with her man, I didn't doubt it.

'I'm flattered, but I'm with Innes.'

'Ah, yes, Innes.'

'Do you have a problem with him?' I dared to ask.

Philippe blinked and then smiled. 'Hopefully not. I like to know who I'm dealing with when it comes to business. I'm planning to invest a lot of money in a venture and so is Innes. But there is something about him. His past isn't available from the usual sources. It's as if he appears on the map only recently. I never trust a man who doesn't have a past.'

'What about your past? Is it squeaky clean and open for all to see?'

He laughed. 'I love your audacity.'

'You're evading the question.'

He laughed again. 'Be aware that I intend to steal you away from Innes if I can. I intend to woo you.'

It was my turn to laugh. 'Woo? You sound like you belong to the era your suit was supposed to be from.'

I thought he was going to stop dancing because he guffawed. Then he said, 'And to answer your question — no my past isn't squeaky clean.'

I nodded firmly. 'See. Everyone is entitled to a grimy past that they want to ignore.'

He smiled and we continued to dance and banter against each other. 'Is there anything that I should know about Innes before I become involved in business with him?'

'No. Nothing at all.' My reply was honest. I didn't want Philippe to know who Innes really was. I hoped the truth came across.

The cold blue eyes tried to emit some genuine warmth. He failed, but full marks for trying. 'I believe you, Bedelia.' He paused. 'Is that your real name?'

'Yes.'

'Don't you have a nickname? Delia perhaps?'

'No. I don't have a shortened version of my name.'

He didn't catch my lie. 'Then I think I'll give you one.' He gazed at my face as if searching for a name that suited me.

'Found a name yet?' I teased him.

'Yes. I'm going to call you Trouble.'

I smiled as I danced with him. If only he'd known he'd made the perfect choice.

Philippe and I sat back down and I ordered from the menu. I trusted that Innes would enjoy the lemon glazed chicken, minted potatoes and seasonal vegetables followed by a classic pudding comprising of fresh fruit, vanilla sponge and cream. Other small courses were included but I kept our order light and fresh.

Polite conversation circulated around the table about nothing that mattered to any of us.

Philippe kept glancing over at me while his dinner date vied occasionally for his attention. She seemed bored and clearly wanted to be elsewhere. I wasn't interested enough to wonder where that would be. My interest was in Innes. Where was he? Our first course was due to be served.

Moments later, Innes came back to the table, apologising for being delayed. 'Business,' he said, as if this explained everything.

Everyone, including Philippe accepted this. Everyone except me.

We ate dinner and chatted amiably.

At one point Philippe went over to another table when he saw an acquaintance he wanted to greet.

I tasted a spoonful of soft sponge, fruit and cream and watched Philippe interact with the man while Innes was called away again for a few minutes.

What would Joyce make of Philippe? I decided to take a sneaky snap of him with my phone. Two of the couples at the table had taken to the dance floor, and I'd no idea where Philippe's lady had gone. I took my phone out and — click. I snapped a picture of him. But the strangest thing happened. Although he couldn't have heard or seen me, Philippe turned and looked right at me, as if sensing I'd done it.

I sent a copy of the picture to Joyce, slipped my phone back into my bag and finished eating my pudding.

Philippe headed back to our table. He was going to saying something. I just knew it.

He sat down next to me. 'Delete the photograph please.'

There was no point in denying I'd snapped it. I put my spoon down, fished my phone out, held the image up so that he could see it and then pressed the delete button.

'Thank you, Bedelia.'

I nodded, put my phone away, picked up my spoon again and continued eating.

He watched me for a moment. 'I don't like having my picture taken without my knowledge.'

I shrugged and took a sip of lemonade. I wanted to keep a clear head so I'd ordered lemonade instead of champagne. No one knew the difference. Served in a champagne glass it looked like the real thing.

This unsettled him. I think he wanted another reaction from me. Well, he was out of luck.

'In my line of work, Bedelia, I have to be careful about my image and where it's distributed. I don't like the idea of casual photographs popping up wherever.'

'What is your line of work?' I'd wanted to ask him this all evening.

'Finance. High finance. I back various business ventures. I provide capital. I'm a risk taker.'

I smiled in disbelief and took another sip of lemonade. 'You don't seem like a risk taker to me.'

He was more intrigued than insulted. 'Why is that?'

'You're all buttoned–up and controlling.' I pressed my hands together as if squeezing the breath out of the air. 'Everything around you is tense. Any risk takers I've ever met have a freedom of arrogance. You seem to be so careful of everything you do and of everyone around you. Look at your attitude towards Innes. And towards me.'

'I've been stung in business many times and I don't like how it feels. I tread carefully.'

'Exactly. That's why you don't seem like a risk taker.'

He nodded, as if I'd trapped him with his own words.

We were quiet for a moment then he said, 'Why did you take a photograph of me?'

'I take pictures all the time. I'm interested in clothing, anything stylish or different. Your suit is different. I wanted a photo of it so that I could look at it later. I'm interested in patterns and designs. Your suit is all wrong and yet...it's so right for you.' I shrugged. 'I'm a dressmaker and designer. Images are part of my work.'

He nodded, accepting my explanation, but he sounded disappointed. 'I had hoped it was because you liked me.'

I did nothing to deter his disappointment.

He lifted my hand and commented on my engagement ring. 'Pretty little ring.'

I pulled my hand away. 'I like it.'

75

'It looks new.'

'It is. I couldn't make up my mind what type of ring I wanted. Innes insisted I choose rather than surprise me with something he liked. I thought I'd like a vintage ring, but then I realised it would have the hopes and dreams of someone else and I changed my mind and decided to have a new ring.'

'A wise choice.'

One of the couples left the dance floor and sat back down at our table.

'Tell me about your designs,' Philippe said to me. 'How do you create them?'

'I draw an illustration of a dress or other item of clothing. Then I start measuring pattern pieces and put a sample of the garment together.'

I sensed that he was still testing me, so I took a pen from my bag and began sketching an evening dress on one of the napkins.

He turned his head to look at my drawing as I worked.

I added lines to the skirt of the dress to show the movement of the fabric. 'Sometimes I alter the neckline as I sketch, changing elements around until it looks like the design I have in mind.'

If anything sold him on my authenticity, this was it.

'You're an amazing woman.' There was no hint of a lie in his voice.

'I'll take that as a compliment coming from a man like you.'

He grinned. 'You don't let me away with anything, do you?'

'Give me two reasons why I should.'

He frowned at me. 'Why two reasons?'

'I like to have more than one option,' I told him. This was also true.

'Great. You may be with Innes, but consider me as another option.'

There was something horribly likeable about him and I couldn't help smiling. I was sure it wouldn't last. He'd say or do something that rubbed my feathers up the wrong way again, but we had our brief exchange of laughter.

That was the moment Innes chose to come back to join us. As my laughter was genuine I sensed that Innes wasn't pleased. But it was his own fault. He'd told me to stick close to him and yet he'd disappeared a few times during the meal.

76

'Oh, I think Innes is angry with us,' Philippe said lightly, making sure Innes heard him.

Innes glared at him as if he wanted to punch him.

Philippe wasn't phased. 'It's your own fault. You should never leave anything precious unattended.'

Innes' lips tightened, and then he said to me, 'Shall we dance?'

I stood up.

'Can I keep this?' Philippe pointed to the napkin I'd drawn the dress illustration on.

'Eh, yes,' I said.

Philippe thrust the pen at me and smiled. 'Sign it for me.' His eyes flicked between Innes and me.

To save any altercation, because there was definitely one brewing, I signed my signature with a quick flourish on the napkin.

Philippe looked at it and smiled, delighted.

Innes cast a glance at the napkin. I could tell that he was worried about what I'd signed as my name. Had I remembered to sign it Bedelia? No, I hadn't.

Philippe folded the napkin and put it in his pocket. 'I'm keeping this,' he said, grinning.

I linked my arm through Innes' arm and let him lead me on to the dance floor. I had a lot of explaining to do — including why I'd signed my name, Trouble.

Dancing with Innes felt so much better than dancing with Philippe and yet I felt the tension in him.

I explained about the Trouble nickname before he had a chance to ask.

Philippe watched us dancing and so we smiled at each other and danced over near the Christmas tree where his view was obscured.

'You weren't supposed to make him like you,' Innes complained.

'I didn't do it deliberately. You shouldn't have kept leaving me on my own.'

He shook his head, annoyed with himself rather than me. 'Well, rein in the charm. Don't be so damned likeable.'

'I've insulted him numerous times,' I said in my defence.

'Yes, but he likes it. You're a breath of fresh air in comparison to the women he dates.'

'Can I help it if I'm a novelty to him?'

'You're more than a novelty, Bee. You're...you're...'

'I'm what?'

He stopped dancing and kissed me.

Everything seemed to pause in that moment.

Then he gazed at me and said, 'Beautiful and intelligent, talented and feisty — and more than a match for him when it comes to crossing verbal swords. That's what I love about you. And now that's what's snared him.'

'What do you want me to do?'

'Pull back. We achieved what we set out to do. He believes we're a couple, that you're my fiancée and that I'm a businessman he's confident to invest his money with.'

'Can we leave now?' I clasped his arms and pulled him close to me. 'Let's just get out of here.'

'We can't risk ruining the impression he has of us. Leaving now would seem wrong and could spark his suspicions again. No, we have to stay for at least another hour. Just don't play into his hands, okay?'

'Okay. I'll try to be like his girlfriend. Sophisticated with a stick up my arse and totally uninterested in him.'

He laughed.

I looked around and saw her standing at the cocktail bar. 'Isn't that her drinking champagne and batting her false eyelashes at another man?'

Innes looked over at her. 'It certainly is.'

'Should I tell Philippe?' I said.

'You're up to mischief. I'm not sure I should condone it.'

'Awe, come on.'

'No, let me tell him. Hopefully that'll keep him occupied.'

We left the dance floor and went over to our table.

'Isn't that your girlfriend over there drinking at the bar and making eyes at another sucker?' Innes chose his words less tactfully than I would've done.

Philippe looked over at her and sneered. 'I was bored with her anyway. She can go home with him.'

'Ain't love wonderful.' The sarcasm in Innes' tone was obvious.

'I think it can be — with the right woman.' Philippe looked at me and then he was swept up in a conversation with two other men who approached him. The back slapping and camaraderie let Innes and me slip away. We went over to one of the other bars and sat down. Innes ordered a glass of champagne. I had lemonade.

'What else has Philippe been saying to you?'

'Apart from giving me a nickname, telling me he intends stealing me away from you, and hating having his photograph taken, that's about it.'

'You asked to take his photograph?'

'No, I didn't ask. I took a sneaky one but he somehow knew I'd done it.'

'You can't mess with men like him. He's shrewd. His pre guesses are more accurate than most people's sure things. That's why he's rich, powerful and a threat if he's allowed free rein to make even more moves. It's my task to make sure that doesn't happen. Unfortunately, I hadn't accounted on him planning to involve you.'

'I'll be back in Glasgow on Monday.'

'Did he ask you where you lived?'

'No, nothing like that. I think he assumes I live in London because we're a couple and this is where you're based. I doubt he thinks we have a long distance relationship.'

'That makes sense. Keep it like that.'

'I will.'

'What did he say to you when you took his photograph?'

'He told me politely to delete it.'

'Did you?'

'Yes. I showed him that I'd deleted it.' I pressed my lips together and sighed. 'But I'd already sent a copy of it to Joyce.'

Innes laughed. 'You really are trouble. Don't even hint that you've got a copy of the photo.'

I zipped my lips which he proceeded to kiss.

We were so engrossed in each other that we didn't notice that Philippe had left the party.

'Damn!' Innes got up and looked around. Philippe had gone. 'Well, at least we can leave now.'

'Thank goodness,' I said. 'If I'd had to drink one more glass of lemonade I'd end up having hiccups all night and into tomorrow.'

We headed out of the function suite and Innes collected my coat for me. 'Are we still going to have lunch on the boat trip?'

'Yes. I'll pick you up at your hotel at eleven in the morning.' He helped me on with my coat. 'I'd love to spend the rest of the evening with you, Bee, but my work's not finished yet.'

'I understand.' Though I wished his work in London was done and we could both go back to Glasgow together. After the boat trip on the River Thames of course. I didn't want to miss out on that.

We stepped outside and I waited at the front of the hotel while Innes drove the car round. The ground sparkled with frost and the sky was a deep winter blue.

There was a sense of snow in the air. I shivered, not from the cold or the thought of the snow, for I loved when it snowed. No, I felt as if I was being watched. I carefully let my eyes scan all around without alerting anyone. If someone was watching me, I didn't want them stepping into the shadows.

But there was no one there.

I shrugged off the feeling and took a deep breath of the fresh night air. Despite all the subterfuge and other nonsense, I had enjoyed myself. My dress had been wonderful to dance in. Nights like this were made for remembering, and I would remember this one I told myself.

Any icy shiver daggered through me and the wind blew through my hair. I brushed it away from my face, and that's when I noticed the engagement ring. I knew I couldn't keep it, and I didn't want to. I'd worry about wearing something that cost a small fortune. Although I'd told Philippe that I wanted a new ring, I would've happily settled for a vintage ring. Nothing that cost as much as the one I was wearing.

Innes drove up and got out to help me into the car. Ever the gentleman. I loved his old–fashioned manners.

Chapter Ten

A Vintage Christmas

When we arrived outside my hotel we sat in the car for a little while talking things over. Then I slipped the ring from my finger and handed it back to him. He put it in his pocket. Neither of us spoke about it, and I preferred it that way. The ring had served its purpose and was no doubt going back to the jeweller he'd borrowed it from, or perhaps the department had borrowed it on his behalf. Whatever the method, the ring wasn't mine to keep. It was all part of the pretence.

'Let's say goodnight here. I'll make my own way up to my room.'

'Thank you, Bee. For everything.'

We kissed goodnight but not goodbye. I'd see him again in the morning.

I walked into the hotel and glanced back through the glass doors as his car drove off into the night. What tasks lay ahead for Innes? I would never know. Perhaps it was easier that way.

'Good evening, Miss,' a member of staff said to me as I walked past the reception towards the lift. 'There's a letter here for you. It was delivered a few minutes ago.'

A letter? For me? I accepted the plain white envelope.

'Will there be a reply, Miss?' he asked.

I opened the hand written letter and read it.

'No, no reply. Thank you.' I went to walk away.

'Goodnight, Miss.'

I hesitated. 'The man who delivered this. Did you see him?'

'Yes. A tall gentleman, dressed for dinner. He had a look about him.'

'Pale blue eyes?'

'Yes, they were very...noticeable,' he said tactfully rather than use the word cold.

'Thank you. Goodnight.'

I stood on the small balcony and gazed out over London with the words of the letter running through my mind.

'If things don't work out between you and Innes, spend Christmas with me in Paris. I think we suit each other. Choose me instead of him.' It was signed, Philippe.

I woke up early the next morning, jarred from a nightmare. It was just after 6:00 a.m.

I jumped in the shower, then got dressed and made a cup of tea.

I sipped my tea and phoned the shop, taking a chance that Joyce would be in. The shop was closed on Sundays but Joyce was often there early to work.

Joyce picked up. 'Morning, Bee.' She'd recognised my number.

'I need you to do something. I sent you a photograph last night.'

'Yes, I got it. You looked lovely in that dress.'

'Thanks, but I was meaning the other photo.'

'Oh the man with the cold eyes.'

'Yes. Please keep that one private. Don't even show Alma until I explain things. And don't send it anywhere else. I'll explain everything when I get back to Glasgow.'

'It's safe with me.'

I didn't doubt it for a second. I loved that I could tell Joyce something and she'd do it on trust without question.

'Thanks, Joyce.'

'Is eh...everything okay?'

'Yes.' I knew she'd understand the hesitant tone in my voice. If anyone could, it was her.

'I'll hear all about it on Monday then.'

'See you then.'

She finished the call without any fuss. Yes, I loved Joyce to bits.

Eleven o'clock arrived in what seemed like a few blinks. Maybe it was the unsettled sleep but I found myself dwelling on events from the previous night and chunks of time were lost deep in thought.

'I'm so glad to see you,' I said to Innes when he arrived. He was casually dressed. Well, as casual as he could be. Everything was black and grey. A black winter coat covered his grey shirt and black trousers. He still looked like money even dressed down on a Sunday.

In total contrast I wore a bright yellow jacket that was cosy and waterproof. I was taking no chances on the weather. Grey skies and spots of rain vied against the sense of snow in the air. I'd dressed warm and sensible. My navy trousers, cream jumper and sturdy ankle boots were up to the task and yet looked quite pretty as an outfit. A pair of mittens that I'd knitted myself were tucked into the pockets of my jacket. They matched the scarf I'd knitted.

I wrapped the scarf around my neck, picked up my bag and off we went.

In the car, I showed him the letter from Philippe. 'I didn't want to show you in the hotel. I'm maybe being paranoid but I thought this would be more private. I couldn't contact you to tell you.' I still didn't have a phone or email number to contact him.

He immediately gave me a phone number. 'Only call if it's something important. They'll patch you through to me.'

I nodded and tried to memorise the number. I'd always had a knack for doing this.

'Who gave you the letter? Was it delivered in person?'

I explained the details of what happened in the hotel reception.

'At the party, did you tell Philippe where you were staying?'

'No, I didn't.'

'He obviously followed us when I drove you back to the hotel after the party.' He sighed heavily. 'I didn't see anyone follow us.'

'Is there something about Philippe you're not telling me? Is he known to be obsessive like this?'

'It's my fault. I shouldn't have involved you. I didn't think he'd be like this. He's known to be obsessive in business. He's never trusted me, and he's right. And he resents me. A clash of personalities. Call it whatever you want, but Philippe hates me, and what better way to put a dagger through my heart than to steal the woman I love.'

'Will I have to fly back to Glasgow today to keep out of his way until all this blows over?'

'No, I'll have to inform my colleagues what's happened. In the meantime, we'll have the day we planned. If, and I doubt it, he's watching the hotel and now watching us, you're safer with me.'

'But I have to go back to Glasgow tomorrow.'

'You will. We'll arrange to leave a trail that will lead Philippe away from where you really are.'

He drove off, driving us to the Thames, constantly checking the rear view mirror. 'There's no sign of anyone following us. He may have been drinking at the party and acted foolishly last night.

Hopefully, we won't have an issue with him, but we'll create a cover for you when you leave London, perhaps letting him think you've gone abroad to a fashion event. Obsessive or not, he'll always put his business before a woman. We'll keep him busy and he'll leave you alone. Besides, if he carries through with the deal with me, we'll net him. That has been our objective.'

The meal on the boat was superb. When I was with Innes everything felt right. I pushed any thoughts of Philippe aside and enjoyed lunch while sailing on the Thames. The weather held steady — wintry cold but dry.

After the meal we sat sipping tea together and enjoyed the spectacular views of the city as we sailed along.

'I've had a wonderful time in London,' I said to Innes.

'I'll be based in Glasgow soon. Then all of this will be in the past.'

'I'm going to sew, design patterns and keep busy so that the time whizzes by.'

He put his arms around my shoulders and hugged me close. 'Not long now, Bee. Not long now.'

It was dark by late afternoon and Innes drove me back to my hotel to collect my things. He told reception that I was leaving early to catch a flight to New York.

Instead, he booked me into another hotel overnight. A hotel that Philippe knew nothing about.

'You'll be safe here tonight,' he assured me.

I nodded, thinking he was leaving and this was goodbye until we met again in Glasgow. But I was wrong. I was safe that night because he stayed with me, watching over me, holding me close until the morning light.

I was whisked away to catch my early morning flight to Glasgow by a trusted acquaintance of Innes. We barely had a chance to kiss goodbye.

We left separately, just in case Philippe was watching Innes. The plan was that Innes would be seen waving someone off at the airport. A woman wearing a bright yellow jacket heading to New York.

I picked up my car from the airport car park in Glasgow and drove straight to the shop. The Christmas tree was lit up in the window. It was one of those dreich, wintry mornings but the festive glow from the shop warmed my heart. I was glad to be home.

Even though there were customers in the shop, Joyce and Alma dropped everything to give me huge welcoming hugs.

I put my case and bags upstairs in the workroom. I hadn't had time to wrap the gifts for Joyce and Alma, so I quickly wrapped them in colourful tissue paper and took them downstairs. I tucked them under the counter until there was a quiet moment in the shop.

Alma opened her present first. 'Oh! Bows for my shoes. These are amazing. I love them. Thank you so much, Bee.'

While Alma interchanged the bows on her shoes, Joyce unwrapped the antique sewing machine brooch I'd bought for her. 'This is perfect.' She pinned it on her cardigan. It had little diamante sparkles on it that caught the light.

Joyce closed the shop a little bit early for lunch. She'd made a pot of vegetable broth and we each had bowls of that with slices of fresh, crusty bread baked by Gilles.

We settled down and I started to tell them all about my trip to London — the photo shoot, filming the video, and eventually I mentioned that I'd been to the dinner dance with Innes.

We chatted and gossiped and caught up with all the news.

Then Joyce whispered to me while Alma was in the kitchen boiling the kettle for more tea, 'What happened with that man in the photograph?'

I gave her the short course of events.

She looked concerned. 'I think we should show Alma what he looks like. It's only fair she should know in case he turns up here at the shop.'

I almost choked. 'You don't think he'll come here, do you?'

'It's doubtful, but men often surprise us women. Alma should see the picture of him.'

'The picture of who?' said Alma, bringing the tea through. 'Is there a man you met you're not telling me about?'

I nodded to Joyce. She pulled up the photo on her phone and held it up to Alma.

Alma screwed her face up. 'Oh, I don't like the look of him.' She peered at him again. 'He's handsome but he gives me a cold feeling. He makes me want to step back.'

'And so you should if you ever see him,' said Joyce. 'He's got a thing about Bee. Hopefully, he's never going to come near her again, but if he does, let me know immediately and don't be alone with him, Alma.'

'Is he dangerous?' she asked.

'He's obsessive,' I told her.

'Is he in Glasgow?'

'No, Alma. He's in London.'

'Phew! The further away the better,' she said.

The remainder of our conversation went back to discussing the photo shoot, the video, the marketing plans for the new designs for the department store, the things that I'd gone to London to deal with. Being with Joyce and Alma again and chatting about our fabrics and fashions, made me feel better. I did miss Innes, but I was glad to be back where I belonged in the shop, steeped in dressmaking and paper patterns.

Chapter Eleven

Fairy Lights & Fashion

We had a busy afternoon serving customers. Our new fabrics, especially the Christmas collection, were selling well.

As the day darkened the shop looked even more Christmassy. Alma really had gone to a lot of bother to drape fairy lights in various parts of the shop. Some of the lights were Christmas classics, including lanterns, Santas and reindeers in glowing rich colours.

Joyce pulled out the robin doorstop she was sewing from under the counter. 'What do you think?' she asked me.

'Very festive. Are you going to sell him?'

'Yes, Alma and I decided to try out a pattern for the doorstop and we've used the robin fabric you designed. The fabric with the large robins on it that customers like to use to make quilts.'

'I've made one too,' said Alma. She brought it over and sat it on the counter.

'They look great. I love things like this. I want to make one.'

Joyce gave me the pattern from her sewing bag. 'I stuffed my robin doorstop with our soft toy filler. Alma stuffed hers with rags and yarn. You can use either. They both work and the finished effect is similar. There's always more than one way to stuff a robin.'

I put the pattern in my bag, cut enough of the robin print fabric to make the doorstop and helped myself to some of the toy filler. 'I'll work on him tonight. I loved when I had a project to make that could be finished in an evening.

Joyce started to lock up the shop after Alma left. Alma's boyfriend arrived most evenings to pick her up.

I tidied up behind the counter while Joyce flicked the overhead lights off until all that lit the shop was the Christmas tree glow and fairy lights.

'It looks magical,' I said to her.

She looked around. 'It does. This will be the first Christmas I've ever had with others helping me in the shop. I'm really looking forward to it. I think we'll have a great time.' Then she became serious. 'Listen, Bee, if you feel nervous on your own at home, at any time until Innes comes back to Glasgow, you're always welcome to stay at my house. Come round any time.'

'Thanks, Joyce. I appreciate the offer. Hopefully I'll be okay and there will be no more trouble from Philippe.'

There was a loud knock on the door. I jumped.

Joyce remained calm. 'It's okay. It's just Gilles. What's that he's flapping at us? A newspaper?' She opened the door and let him in.

'Have you seen the newspaper?' He scrambled to open it at the page he wanted us to see. 'And welcome back, Bee. Glad to see you home again.' He flicked through the pages and then spread the paper on the counter so we could read it.

I gasped. 'Oh my goodness. It's me! The marketing people didn't tell me they were going ahead with the press release for the new designs so quickly.'

'You're in the paper, Bee. You look lovely. And they've featured our fabrics.' Joyce pointed to the photographs. There were three photos with captions and an editorial. It was the main feature in the fashion news section.

'What a splash of publicity,' I said, my heart pounding with excitement.

Joyce's glasses looked like they were due to steam up. 'Do we need to do anything?' She glanced around the shop. 'Do we have enough stock, enough of the fabrics?'

I studied the photos and read the feature. 'Everything that's been mentioned we already have in stock, though it would be worthwhile to order more of the Christmas fabrics, the dancing people prints and maybe a few others.' I could hear the rising excitement in my voice.

'I've only just had a chance to read the paper,' said Gilles. 'This came out as an early evening edition here.'

'We'll need to be in sharp tomorrow to get ready in case we're extra busy,' said Joyce. 'I'll phone Alma and tell her the news.'

Joyce couldn't wait to get home. 'I'm sure I have some fabric stock at home that I can bring in tomorrow.'

'I'll lock up,' I offered.

'Great, thanks, Bee. See you in the morning, bright and early.' And off she went, leaving me with Gilles.

'You can keep that copy of the paper,' he said. 'The chances are this feature was out in the London papers all day. Believe me I know these things. I've had to deal with the press and newspaper promotions for years.'

Gilles' words jolted me as I realised it was a possibility that my photo and work location had been circulated in London since the morning. I wouldn't be able to phone the marketing team until the following day to find out.

Gilles was about to leave me to lock up when a face peered in the shop window. I shuddered when I saw him. What the hell was Philippe doing here? Then I realised. Oh no. He'd read about me in the paper.

He smiled coldly at me through the window.

Gilles' phone rang. It was an urgent call. 'Sorry to leave you. Shout if that guy bothers you. I have to take this call, Bee.'

I wondered what to do. 'Can you wait with me for a minute?'

'Yes.'

I remembered Innes' number and made an urgent call. I got through immediately but they said Innes was already on a call. 'Tell him that Philippe is here at the shop in Glasgow.' I heard by their manner that they understood. They promised to inform the police and have someone there as soon as possible. I hung up.

I nodded again to Gilles and then followed him outside. He hurried into his coffee shop, talking angrily into his phone, dealing with whatever problem had arisen with his business.

I stood outside the dress shop and spoke to Philippe, somehow feeling safer talking to him there. No way was I going to let him inside the shop.

'What do you want, Philippe?' I tried to sound strong, unafraid of him.

'You lied to me, Bedelia. Or should I say, Bee? Or did I name you well when I called you Trouble?'

'I'll do what the hell I want. I'm not answerable to you.'

He stepped closer. I wanted to step back but that would show fear so I stood my ground.

'I like a woman who has a daring attitude,' he said.

He reached out to touch me.

'Keep away from me,' I warned him. 'I don't want anything to do with you.'

He glared at me and then pulled his phone out and made a call. He spoke in French. I didn't understand a word of it.

Then he walked away.

I shivered, tugging my cardigan around me, but the coldness I sensed from him was icier than the freezing night air.

Gilles came running out to me. He seemed to have just finished making another phone call. 'Are you okay, Bee?'

I nodded while watching the tall figure walk away along the street.

'Do you know what that man said on the phone?' said Gilles.

'No, I don't understand a word of French.' But of course Gilles knew. He was fluent in French.

'He said that he was going to deal with you,' Gilles told me. 'He sounded very resentful. Do you want me to phone the police?'

'Thanks, Gilles, but the police are on their way.'

'Do you want to come in and wait in my shop?' he offered.

'No, it's fine. I'm going to go into the shop and lock the door.'

'Okay, I'm right next door if you change your mind.'

I went inside, locked the door, checked it was secure and then went upstairs to put my coat on, hoping it would warm me up, though I was no doubt suffering from shock.

I put the lights on in the workroom and kept a lookout for the police. Where were they?

I turned away from the window when I heard a noise from the stockroom. No, Philippe couldn't have climbed in the back window. Could he? My blood turned cold when I realised he had.

'You don't seem pleased to see me, Bee,' he said, stepping out of the darkness of the storeroom into the workroom area.

I glanced at the stairs. I couldn't make a run for it. He was standing too close to the staircase.

Then I heard the shop door open downstairs and Joyce called up to me. 'Bee, where are you? Are you upstairs?'

'Don't come up,' I shouted to her. But it was too late. She was already hurrying up the stairs. She stopped when she saw Philippe standing there. He didn't appear to be armed, but his presence was threatening enough.

Philippe turned his anger towards me. 'Why you little...' He lunged at me, but suddenly Joyce appeared to stumble and fall against one of the clothes rails. It fell between us, thankfully preventing Philippe from grabbing me.

What happened next was a complete blur because the lights, all of them, went out. I heard a rumbling noise, a scuffle, then the sound of someone tumbling down the stairs and a dull thud when they landed.

'Joyce,' I screeched. 'Joyce, are you okay?'

'Yes,' she said, standing right beside me.

My eyes became accustomed to the dark and the light from the street lit up her face. A shadowy figure lay unconscious downstairs.

I threw my arms around Joyce. 'Thank goodness you're okay. I thought he'd hurt you and thrown you down the stairs.'

'No, I'm fine. He must've stumbled in the dark and fallen down himself.'

The flash of police car lights flickered through the window.

'The police have arrived,' I said, wary to go downstairs in case Philippe still had some fight in him. Thankfully the police arrested him. He moaned and groaned as they led him away. I peered outside, watching the police put him into the back of a car.

The shop lights suddenly went back on.

'The fuses are overloaded with all the fairy lights,' said Joyce. 'I shouldn't have let Alma put up so many.'

We went down and talked to the police who had the situation under control. Whatever Innes' people in London had told them, I didn't need to make a statement and neither did Joyce. I seemed surprised. She didn't. Oh to have her attitude.

And then I wondered about Joyce... She had the ability to size people up at a glance. She'd advised me not to photograph anyone at the dinner dance in London. The advice she gave me was very discerning. I liked her discretion.

Joyce had made a pot of tea. 'You're upset. I can see how pale you look, dear. But everything will be okay now. Thankfully Gilles had the sense to phone me and tip me off about that man so I could come back here. Though the police would've arrived to help you.'

'Is Gilles who I think he is? Is he really the coffee shop owner? Nothing more than that?'

'He is. Gilles lives in a world of cakes and baking.'

'And what about you, Joyce? What about your world?' She knew exactly what I was asking her.

She set our cups up for tea. 'Everyone has a past.'

'Was yours always dressmaking and knitting?'

She shook her head, sighed and sat down at the kitchen table. I poured our tea and sat down opposite her.

'It seems like a lifetime ago,' she began. 'And in a way it is. I was just a girl in my twenties in London looking for a job. I started work for a Government office and they found that I had a knack for understanding codes and people.'

'You were a code breaker? A profiler?'

She shrugged. 'We didn't call it that. But, yes, I suppose I was. Not for long. The job wasn't for me. I prefer my sewing and knitting, though I did have a special talent for knitting that was useful.'

'So what really happened upstairs? Did you stumble and fall against the clothes rail?'

'I thought he was going to hit you, so I made sure he didn't.'

We smiled at each other.

'And the fairy lights? They didn't cause everything to fuse?'

'No. This shop could take twice as many lights and not fuse anything. I flicked the lights off and booted his arse down the stairs.'

I looked at her and smiled. 'Cheers, Joyce.'

She tipped her cup against mine. 'Cheers, Bee.'

'I've never been involved with anything from my past since I left,' she said. 'When I walked away from the past, that's where I left it. My shop has been my life all these years and that's what I'm interested in.'

'I won't tell anyone. I won't even tell Innes.'

She smiled. 'Innes knows fine well. He's not daft, Bee.'

I was pleased that he knew. There would be no deep secrets between us. But Joyce was right. The past was over. No raking over the old coals for us.

Two weeks before Christmas Innes left his past in London and started his new life in Glasgow — with me.

Joyce even knitted him a Christmas present, a jumper. I wasn't sure about the pattern on the front. It was sort of knobbly but nice. She promised to teach me her knitting technique.

Instead of wrapping his present, she put it on one of the mannequins in the front window. 'I'd like him to see it there. I think he'll appreciate it. And customers can see how lovely our new yarn knits up.'

And so Innes' red jumper was on display beside the Christmas tree in the shop window. Customers did like it and bought up the yarn.

He hadn't been to the shop yet to see it. Every spare minute he was working, settling in to the Glasgow office. He seemed to love it there and had no regrets about leaving London and his old life behind. Besides, he still worked for the Government but in an office–based capacity. No daring exploits for him these days. He was also busy getting our new house ready for Christmas. I would've been happy to move into his fancy apartment, or have him come and live with me, but he could afford to buy us a house in a leafy area of the city and took pride in making a sewing room for me with plenty of wardrobes wherever I wanted them. Yes, I'd met the man who was made for me.

A few days before Christmas it started snowing. The city was iced to perfection. Glasgow's beautiful architecture looked even more magnificent frosted and covered in snow, like something out of a fairytale wonderland. The shops in the city centre sparkled with Christmas cheer and traditional carols played alongside modern festive music.

Innes said he'd pick me up at night outside the shop. I'd been working late, sewing, knitting, sorting out last minute repairs to the dresses — and making robin doorstops. Yes, they were popular with customers. And there was definitely more than one way to stuff a robin.

I put my coat on when I saw him drive up. Alma and Joyce had just left and I said I'd lock up.

I hurried outside. It had been snowing all day. My boots crunched into the snow and the cold, fresh air filled me with a sense of anticipation. I was looking forward to having dinner with Innes. I enjoyed having dinner with him every evening.

Flakes of snow drifted down, highlighted against the glow of the streetlamps.

Innes had the collar of his coat turned up. He smiled at me and yet he looked nervous.

'Is something wrong?' I asked him, standing on booted tip toes to kiss him.

'No. Everything's fine, but there's something missing.' He produced a ring from his pocket. A sparkling diamond ring. Not

93

unlike the one I'd worn in London. This one looked a bit more traditional in its design. He held my hand and then he said, 'I love you, Bee. Will you marry me?'

Through tears of joy I murmured, 'Yes.'

He put the ring on my finger. It sparkled as the snow fell all around us. 'I had it designed for you. I hope you like it.'

'I love it, Innes. It's perfect.' I threw my arms around him and told him how much I loved him too.

'Come on,' he said, 'let's get some dinner.'

We went to walk away but he noticed the jumper in the shop window.

'That's your Christmas jumper. Joyce knitted it for you, but she hoped it would be okay to display it for customers to see it.'

He laughed as he looked at the jumper.

I frowned.

He smiled and walked over to have a closer look at it. He nodded and laughed again. 'Merry Christmas to you too, Joyce,' he said.

'What do you mean?'

He pointed to the pattern on the front of the jumper. 'Don't you know what it says?'

'What it says?'

'Yes, she's knitted a message in Morse Code.'

'Really?' I tried to see what he saw but it looked like a knobbly stitch to me. 'What does it say?'

'It says — Merry Christmas.'

I smiled. 'She assures me that your secrets and mine are safe with her.'

He nodded. 'I don't doubt that.'

He put his arm around my shoulder. 'Come on, let's go home. I think we have something to celebrate.'

I looked at the engagement ring on my hand as the snow sprinkled around us on that special night. He leaned down and kissed me, and then we headed home together.

End

About the Author:

Follow De-ann on Instagram @deann.black

De-ann Black is a bestselling author, scriptwriter and former newspaper journalist. She has over 80 books published. Romance, crime thrillers, espionage novels, action adventure. And children's books (non-fiction rocket science books and children's fiction). She became an Amazon All-Star author in 2014 and 2015.

She previously worked as a full-time newspaper journalist for several years. She had her own weekly columns in the press. This included being a motoring correspondent where she got to test drive cars every week for the press for three years.

Before being asked to work for the press, De-ann worked in magazine editorial writing everything from fashion features to social news. She was the marketing editor of a glossy magazine. She is also a professional artist and illustrator. Fabric design, dressmaking, sewing, knitting and fashion are part of her work.

Additionally, De-ann has always been interested in fitness, and was a fitness and bodybuilding champion, 100 metre runner and mountaineer. As a former N.A.B.B.A. Miss Scotland, she had a weekly fitness show on the radio that ran for over three years.

De-ann trained in Shukokai karate, boxing, kickboxing, Dayan Qigong and Jiu Jitsu. She is currently based in Scotland.
Her colouring books and embroidery design books are available in paperback. These include Floral Nature Embroidery Designs and Scottish Garden Embroidery Designs.

Also by De-ann Black (Romance, Action/Thrillers & Children's books). See her Amazon Author page or website for further details about her books, screenplays, illustrations, art and fabric designs.
www.De-annBlack.com

Romance books:

Sewing, Crafts & Quilting series:
1. The Sewing Bee
2. The Sewing Shop

Quilting Bee & Tea Shop series:
1. The Quilting Bee
2. The Tea Shop by the Sea

Heather Park: Regency Romance

Snow Bells Haven series:
1. Snow Bells Christmas
2. Snow Bells Wedding

Summer Sewing Bee
Christmas Cake Chateau

Cottages, Cakes & Crafts series:
1. The Flower Hunter's Cottage
2. The Sewing Bee by the Sea
3. The Beemaster's Cottage
4. The Chocolatier's Cottage
5. The Bookshop by the Seaside

Sewing, Knitting & Baking series:
1. The Tea Shop
2. The Sewing Bee & Afternoon Tea
3. The Christmas Knitting Bee
4. Champagne Chic Lemonade Money
5. The Vintage Sewing & Knitting Bee

The Tea Shop & Tearoom series:
1. The Christmas Tea Shop & Bakery
2. The Christmas Chocolatier
3. The Chocolate Cake Shop in New York at Christmas
4. The Bakery by the Seaside
5. Shed in the City